READY..STEADY..
EXIT

READY..STEADY.. *EXIT*

P C Balasubramanian

Srishti
PUBLISHERS & DISTRIBUTORS

Srishti Publishers & Distributors
N-16, C. R. Park
New Delhi 110 019
editorial@srishtipublishers.com

First published by
Srishti Publishers & Distributors in 2015

10 9 8 7 6 5 4 3 2 1

All characters in this book are fictitious, and any resemblance to real persons, living or dead, is purely coincidental.

The author asserts the moral right to be identified as the author of this work.

Printed and bound in India

To my wife Sunita who married a CA who completed the course after a few failures and who had just set up a small professional entity.

To the highly reputed and valuable Institute of Chartered Accountants of India that produces eminent professionals year after year and creates huge opportunities for them to thrive.

A note from the author

All the narration, opinions and situations are fictional and my own. If I have inadvertently hurt anyone's feelings or profession, I shall feel very sad and here are my apologies in advance. If there is over dosage of filter coffee, Rajinikanth and cricket, am sorry, I grew up with these and would stay addicted to them till I exist on this planet. My objective is to share a light-hearted, interesting and a reasonably meaningful story layered with humour, drama, satire, romance and twists. If you love it, thanks to you, else, give me another chance.

Statutory warning: A few scenes where the characters drink liquor have been included to add charm to the story and make it look realistic. The intention is not to endorse or promote drinking; we know you are capable of handling it by yourself :-)

Acknowledgements

There is no better way than quoting William Arthur Ward to emphasize the importance of expressing gratitude and acknowledge the help rendered and wishes offered by many in my first attempt in scripting a fiction.

"Feeling gratitude and not expressing it is like wrapping a present and not giving it."– William Arthur Ward

Though I have two successful and bestselling books to my credit as a lead author, this is my debut as a fiction writer. I sincerely thank all my well-wishers and friends who were instrumental in propelling me to go ahead with my first attempt with fiction. I must thank them profusely as I realized while scripting this story that 'fiction writing' is joyful, addictive and equally challenging.

My special thanks to all at Srishti Publishers, who agreed to publish my book with an amount of zeal (despite knowing that I didn't have any other option) that would enthuse any writer!

I specially thank my wife Sunita and my two sons Arjun and Jayanth as they were the first ones to read my manuscript not just once, but every time some changes were made to it. They ensured that they didn't disappoint my expectation and each time they could come with different expressions that denoted excitement and approval.

My very special thanks to ICAI and to my many CA friends, without whom life wouldn't have been so challenging and fun –

challenging till I completed the course, and fun after completing it.

I thank in advance all my readers who chose to buy books from conventional stores and online stores instead of borrowing from their friends not to just read this book but also to gift others.

I thank the press and media who are also a reason for this book as there were questions now and then on what could be my next project. I sincerely thank them for the amount of write-ups, articles and even interviews published for my earlier books.

I thank social media for giving the first best option to market and promote the book with no cost attached to it.

On a serious note, hope you are *ready* to plunge into the book, *steady* having fun, and I hope you don't *exit* till you complete reading the book.

I would love to read your views about the book. You could write to me at bala@pcbala.com or write2pcbala@gmail.com. For more information, you can also visit www.pcbala.com.

Love
P C Balasubramanian (Bala)

Jan 2002

There were four months I wished I could erase from my calendar – May and November were the months in which I appeared for my CA exams and January and July the months when I had to face the wrath because of the results. These were the very months I had loved when I had completed my CA Inter exams a couple of years before. But the final exams showed me the bitter side – I used to wonder why the results had to be binary in nature – PASS or FAIL. Shouldn't there have been another option?

I remember one particular day out of those dreadful days – 15 January. It was a week before the result was to be announced. I was visiting my parents in Pondicherry for the Pongal holidays. More than any sentimental reasons, it was the urge to have good food that took me there. Though there were many affordable mess and restaurants available in Chennai, nothing could beat mother's cooking.

My mom was, as usual, extremely enthusiastic to see me and commenced with her customary question as to why I had lost weight! It was not true since I had gained weight, thanks to the only affordable combination of Old Cask Rum and Thums Up. Dad, not unexpectedly, was not as enthused.

Immediately after a sumptuous lunch, my dad was quick to launch on his favourite topic. "I hope you will clear your final exams and settle down."

"Dad, I am not a cyclone victim to settle down now. I have written the exams well, but can't guarantee a favourable result."

"How long, Gautam? We are also becoming old..."

"I know you are becoming old, but you are not the one who is writing the papers."

"Enough of your jokes! You are twenty-six years old now and have not still completed your education! When are you going to start earning seriously?"

"Dad, I am partly employed now. I still work for my firm and manage my expenses. I also want to complete my CA and move on in life!"

"You have been saying this for the last two years. Look at your friends, Dinesh, Anand and Sambu! They cleared their CA in their first attempt and Dinesh is very well employed in Singapore."

My dad's BP was shooting up and so was mine.

"What can I do? Even some of your classmates retired from a much higher position, we never questioned you." For a moment, I thought I had argued really well.

"Did you hear that, Lakshmi?" My dad took on my mom. "You have spoiled him; you have pampered him to the hilt right from his school days and now look at the results!"

"Leave him alone! He has always done well in his studies. It is just that the planetary positions are not favourable for him. We need to wait till the next *Shani Peyarchi* (the planetary movement of Saturn from one house to another plays a significant role in horoscope analytics).

"He is our only son! Mind how you speak to him!" My mom never lost hope in me. Like most moms in the world, she considered her son as the best in class product.

I was not to be outdone. "Dad, I will leave now and see you only after I am a qualified CA. Mark this date in your calendar," the Rajini in me delivered a powerful punch line.

"Then you may not see me till I die," the Amrish Puri in my dad was quick to reply with a dirty grin on his face.

Mom unfailingly used her biggest weapon – she started crying. But my dad ignored her with great ease, coming out of years of practice. I left home in a huff. But though I was angry with my dad, I was also disappointed with myself. Was I useless? Was I unlucky? Was I not focused? Was I not intelligent? Could I change the planetary position right away? My results in the positive could seal all these doubts.

I took the next bus back to Chennai, shedding silent tears. Dinesh, Anand and Sambu were still great friends, but such comparisons drew the 'Lakshman rekha' between us for no fault of theirs. Had I opted for an engineering course, I would have been an engineer by then. But fate had a different plan for me, I thought, and it had decided my calling. It gave me a different message, and in my ears it was sounding clearly like this. I still remember the words reverberating in my mind, "Hey Gautam, you won't win a race without jumping over the hurdles. For you, CA is the only weapon in your arsenal... You will get it sooner or later." My mom was the only other person who supported me, or at least understood my feelings.

As I was travelling from Pondicherry to Chennai, I remembered the time and circumstances that had made me get into this rat trap called CA. After all, there was no one interesting in the fifteen-year-old state-owned bus for me to focus and by default my thoughts went back to 1997.

After completing my B.Com in Pondicherry with outstanding grades, I had to decide the next step that would decide the course of my life. Left to me, I would have pursued M.Com and M.Phil and would have become a reasonably good professor. I always thought that professors had ample time for themselves.

But I succumbed to peer pressure like many others, and to add to that, my dad's friend's daughter Neha too joined the CA course in Pondicherry. She was a brilliant student and, more importantly, she was beautiful. I always felt inadequate around her. She was immensely knowledgeable about corporate and economic affairs and discussed her views with me. I used to wonder if her intent to pour out her knowledge and awareness when I was around was to impress me or suppress me. My massive knowledge was restricted to two great aspects of India – cinema and cricket. Unfortunately, my knowledge from BS Chandrasekhar to Ian Botham, from Lara to Sachin and Saurav, and from Shivaji Ganesan to Kamal Hassan and Rajinikanth was wasted on my peer group. A bit of irrelevant and misplaced ego also occupied the excess, unused space in my mind since I never used my mind beyond minimum required. I was a bit annoyed with Neha too. 'Why should beautiful girls have brilliant minds too!' I had to prove a point that I could also become a CA. Yet, I decided to move out of Pondicherry to Chennai as I didn't want to be in the same place where Neha also pursued her course. She would obviously outperform me and my male ego would depreciate at a faster pace. I didn't mind my ego falling flat against her beauty, but not against her knowledge and success.

Hence I decided to move to Chennai, immensely happy to escape the constant supervision of my nagging dad, but certainly unhappy to let Neha out of sight – a decision I regret till today. Being a Tamil cinema buff, I should have proposed to her then. In most movies, brilliant or rich girls always fell for unemployed, good-for-nothing heroes. But since I didn't do it then, professional education shifted me from Pondicherry to Chennai – away from the beauty and the beast!

But I was not the only one to shift to Chennai. My great friend Anand too joined me and we were really excited about living in a new place. Of course, our parents made up for the long distance by giving us their quota of thousand pieces of advice in one shot.

Anand did not suffer from the danger of being complimented for his looks. He was a bit short, a bit fat. His style would never catch on as a trend. But mercifully, his looks did not bother him. What he lacked in the looks department, he more than made up for with astute knowledge, work culture and dedication. He had a golden heart that could melt anyone. He was tolerant, soft spoken and calm.

Quite my opposite, one could say. I cared about the way I looked, the way I presented myself and my positioning. My height of almost six feet, marginally dusky complexion and a near perfect physique roused the interest of the fairer sex. While I got complimented for my looks, my work left much to desire for. My superior customer management skills came to my rescue. I was a king among beggars, thanks to this.

Anand knew people in Chennai, so we were lucky to get accommodation in a small apartment in Triplicane – a bachelor's paradise since there were many *mami* mess (small food joints run by south Indian Brahmin ladies) and other eateries.

Anand and I managed to join a CA firm for articleship. During this period, one had to undergo training under a CA for three years and handle a lot of work while also simultaneously preparing for the exams – a strong cocktail recipe that clearly signified the red signal for ordinary students like me. I never understood why a CA firm always had many serious and sad faces and even dull-looking books decorated with dust. The mystery was cleared as I stared blankly at Ramaiah's *The Companies Act 1956* on one of the partners' table. I could feel butterflies in my stomach. 'Do I have to study this book? I will surely not complete this till I am in my grave,' I thought. If I died because of depression, fear or other psychological factors,

I will hold Mr. Ramaiah responsible for this, I vowed to myself! This brought me a brief respite of amusement. I presumed Neha thought of it as a great book of bed time stories. Before I had left Pondicherry, Neha had told me as we parted that she might need my help in getting reference books from Chennai. I was disappointed that she did not seem to regret my leaving. She could have at least told me to stay in touch.

I somehow managed to navigate through the interview. I had to sound very ambitious about wanting to become a CA so that I was selected.

"Guys, CA is a very tough course and you need to study for five hours every day," my boss said.

It was like being hit by a missile the moment the war was declared. More shocks awaited me.

"If you don't," he continued ominously, glaring each one in the eye meaningfully, "you will remain a B.Com even after five years." He was blunt and frank. He topped this with the most irrelevant information – that he secured the fifteenth rank in the inter exams and thirty-first in the final exams.

His prophecy almost came true. He could have become a successful astrologer, I realized, except that instead of two parrots inside a miniature cage, he had two fat books on top of the table. Looking at him and his musty office, I thought that rank holders didn't necessarily succeed in their profession.

Anand and I succeeded in securing admission for the articleship. Thankfully, we were not the only two guinea pigs; there were a few more. Most of them looked as though they were born to study and secure ranks. They seemed to prefer the likes of Ramaiah to the likes of Neha.

A sudden jolt from the brakes and a screeching sound brought me back to the present and I realized we had reached Chennai. I got down from the bus and had to negotiate with an auto driver for fifteen minutes before we agreed on the fare. I always believed that the best training for any procurement manager would be in Chennai if he was asked to deal with and negotiate with the auto drivers day after day for a period of sixty days. Apart from tolerance, one could learn negotiation skills and a fair amount of lewd Tamil.

A message from Anand beeped just then. He was waiting with an Old Cask rum and Thums Up bottle, and this elevated my mood immediately!

We had shifted from Triplicane to T. Nagar as Anand, after he qualified in his first attempt, joined an automobile manufacturing company in the Finance and Accounts department. Since he had a proper job, we could afford a better apartment at a higher rent.

Anand was not only brilliant and extremely organised, but he was also an avid learner and got into micro details even about dry subjects. I was very macro as I had no patience for details. The result was self-evident – Anand cleared his exams in the first attempt and started earning while I was still learning.

Neha too had cleared her exams and the Great Wall of China rose between us. Why would she care for the likes of me? Since her success and my failure, we had lost touch with each other. With great hopes I had applied for the post of Assistant Commercial Manager in a large MNC foods company eight months ago. The advertisement had clearly mentioned that even CA finalists (the rats trying to escape the trap) could also apply as there were many openings in the company for that post. I didn't understand why they needed so many commercial managers to deal with chocolates and beverages. Either the existing ones in the company had put in their papers or they were not doing their jobs properly.

Meanwhile, I didn't clear my finals despite what I thought was a good performance. The Costing paper cost me my success yet again, pulling me down from the virtual heights I had imagined I had achieved. I decided that I would engage a qualified Cost Accountant under me some day and indirectly take revenge against the very subject that had been pulling down me, my ego, my dream, every six months.

Before entering the room in a hotel where this interview was being conducted, I started praying to all the gods. I realized that I had totally ignored some of these gods in the last few months. I promised I would make amends and pleaded with these gods not to take revenge on me.

The interview was informal and I started feeling very comfortable in the first proper interview of my life. The interviewer was interrupted by a call and he stepped out, gesturing me to wait. A man's mind travels very fast in fantasy world. The way the interview was proceeding, I was already imagining myself in my second or third month of employment – a good salary, fab cubicle, centrally air conditioned floor with bright posters, designer rest rooms with a lovely fragrance that motivate you to have more number of bio breaks than required, two attractive girls directly reporting to me and discreetly admiring me, a beautiful residential apartment close to a high street, and single malt whiskey replacing the good old rum in my mini bar. In this extremely colourful and delightful scene, the only jarring note was the spread sheet on my laptop screen, and I shivered when I also thought of the possibility of having to report to Neha one day. But before this dream could prolong, the interviewer came in and brought me back to reality.

He was visibly glowing as a big smile covered his face and I doubted if that was a call from his girl.

"So, Gautam, you are from Pondicherry… What is so special about that place?"

"Good educational institutions, the French culture, beautiful heritage buildings, quality health care facilities, the Aurobindo Ashram, Auroville and mmm..." Neha also came to my mind, but I didn't think that would be relevant here.

"Come on Gautam, liquor is very cheap out there I believe...?"

Was this a trick question? I replied carefully, underplaying my interest in that subject.

The last question was very easy but the answer was very complicated.

"Gautam, now that results are out, I hope you have passed."

"No sir, there is no change in my resume." I couldn't meet his eyes when I replied, but I was pleased that I had managed to convey subtly the fact that I had *failed*. I realized this was my strength – using words appropriately even in the most difficult situations.

"Sorry Gautam, as per our company policy, we can hire only qualified accountants. My advice to you is apply again after you clear next time."

"I will do it. My request to you is that you don't forget to call me again." I shook his hand and left the room with a heavy heart and a superficial smile.

My breathing returned to normal when I reached home and Anand opened the door with his customary cool smile. "So how was your trip? Hope your parents blessed you with a favourable result..." Anand was curious to know. My silence was enough; after all, he had known me for years.

"Did you meet Neha? How is she?" he shot another question unexpectedly.

"I don't care for her, don't you know?" For a moment, I really meant it, though the next moment I wanted to take back my words!

"But she does," Anand winked.

Imagine a cricketer in a one day match, missing the last ball when he needed just two runs to win, and suddenly the umpire declares it a 'no ball'! My elation was akin to that lucky batsman.

"What are you saying?" I asked puzzled, scared to have my hopes crashed.

"Yea, she called me and conveyed her best wishes to you. She said she would meet you after you clear your exams," Anand said with a twinkle in his eyes.

Whether it was true or not, I got into a frenzied mood. Her call seemed like an omen, suggesting I would be becoming a full-fledged Chartered Accountant very soon.

"How did she call you? Are you guys in touch?" I wanted to know.

"She has my number and she enquires about you every time we talk. She likes you and who knows, she may be in love with you." Anand raised my expectations. For me, this was like securing an all India rank in CA.

"Really, bastard, you never told me anything all these days, not even when you were drunk!" I chided him affectionately.

"She didn't want to distract or disturb you, so I promised not to say anything. Don't worry, from now on, your fortunes are changing for the better. Let us drink to that." I hugged him.

We were into the third peg. I was certainly drinking faster that evening.

"Gautam, what do you intend doing after completing CA? Do you plan to continue in the same firm for a while longer? Will they make you a partner later?" Anand could still think straight.

I shook my head. "I don't intend continuing in this firm. I want to move on...and more later. Fix me another drink and let me go to bed. I don't want anything to disturb my mind as it is filled with thoughts of Neha." I grinned.

"Oh sure, I understand. Sleep well. Another week and we will party hard after your results." Anand wished me good night with these positive words. I went to bed to attempt to sleep, because life seemed full of attempts till then for me!

I was floating in happiness, excitement and joy as thoughts of Neha – her brilliance, her maturity, her concern for me – circled in my head. Did it mean she cared for me more than as a mere friend? What did she like about me – my looks, my personality, my intelligence, or lack of it? But through it all, I could also sense a nagging worry about my results in one corner of my mind.

The combined power of the two extreme emotions should have kept me awake, but thanks to the good old rum, I went into deep sleep.

♌

Two Days Before the Results

Anand was travelling to Mumbai for work. I left for office with great reluctance as most of the discussions amongst the prospective CAs would be 'results' and 'things to do post results'. But I could not stay home since I had to discuss work with the boss. A client was complaining that we auditors, particularly me, were not competent enough to make sure he paid less tax despite our best efforts in reducing the tax impact by booking several expenses. At times I had to even do the dirty job of requesting the client not to book his child's diaper expenses under 'staff welfare' expenses. He compared himself with his younger brother who, in a similar line of business, did more sales and paid less tax. He was envious of his younger brother who was married to a more beautiful girl from a very rich family. Though they were not on talking terms, they had access to each other's financial data through common contacts. I had to deal with such lousy accounts that I lost all passion for my work.

That day, my boss Mr. Venugopal was in a good mood. Maybe he had received long-pending dues or one of his planned personal trips was going to be converted into an official one.

"Good morning, sir."

"Good morning, Gautam. All the very best for your results. I am sure you will get through this time. After all, this is the fifth year of your CA..."

Mr. Venugopal was always good with numbers and had good memory on account of clean habits! He liked to display accurate knowledge at all times, regardless of its relevance to the situation.

"Thanks, sir. I certainly hope to pass this time," I said, wanting to end the conversation quickly.

"In case you don't, you need not worry. I will promote you as our Senior Audit Manager and you can handle accounts that don't need a qualified CA."

What a considerate man, I couldn't help thinking sarcastically. I managed to stretch my lips to a smile. Maybe encouraged, he continued relentlessly, "Anand was really brilliant and an outstanding student. He cleared all his papers in his first attempt. Doesn't matter, it happens... In fact, those days my neighbour Santhanam and I joined CA together and even after twelve attempts, he didn't pass. He finally changed lines...," he guffawed merrily. "You need some intelligence and hard work to be a CA." He was not trying to make a friend of me, I could make out.

For all we know, Santhanam could be running a more profitable and larger business today, since he did not say anything about what Santhanam was doing then.

I left his cabin and spent a few minutes with my colleagues and students. The colleagues were like me, continuing in the firm as they hadn't cleared their CA exam; and students were the ones who had just completed their articleship and had appeared for the final exams. The body language clearly communicated tension. We tended to become introverts for a few days ahead of the results; such climate changes happened every six months.

Luckily I was respected by the students and colleagues because my clients respected me. My boss had always openly appreciated my client management skills and that I could learn the art of dealing with the regulatory authorities too under his guidance.

He had reasons to acknowledge my client relationship management skills. A few months back, one of his partners quit the firm to form his own entity and he even managed to take with him a few clients who were directly serviced by him. This jolted Mr. Venugopal. I took the responsibility of meeting every client of his as a precautionary measure against their migration to the new entity set up by an erstwhile partner. I didn't stop here. I initiated a new practice in the firm where a monthly newsletter was launched for the benefit of our clients on the latest case studies and even business opportunities relevant to most of them. In addition to that, since we had the data on the commencement date of the business of each of our clients, each of them was sent a bouquet with a personal letter from Mr. Venugopal wishing them on that day! This was not only well received and helped strengthen the relationship with the clients, but also enabled an increase in the fee for some clients. Most times, simple initiatives result in magnifying the morale of clients and employees.

A couple of hours after lunch, I informed my boss that I wouldn't be attending office the next day and left for the day.

I reached home and called my parents. My dad, who knew that the results would be published in the next couple of days, politely wished me success and advised me to visit the Sai Baba temple in Mylapore. I was surprised at how calm he sounded! Either he had given up on me or it was the calm before the storm. My mom was her usual self. She wished me success and told me that many less intelligent people have passed the course and that I would definitely clear it. Even at such a trying time, I wondered from where she could get the data to pass such a judgment. Mothers don't need authentic and validated data to praise their children!

I spoke to Anand, who was returning on the day of the result. He was surer of my success; perhaps he had great belief in the law of probability. I wanted to take Neha's number from him but something said (what else, it was the bloody inferiority complex) that I should talk to her only after I was a qualified professional – *a complete man* – to borrow the tagline from Raymond.

♌

The Day of the Result! 21 January

I got up early in the morning, at around 5.30, and after taking a shower, left the apartment to visit as many temples as possible till ten in the morning and have a sumptuous breakfast (mini-tiffin) at Hotel Saravana Bhavan. Anand was expected in the evening and he had assured me he would accompany me, for the first time, to the institute to check my results.

I started with Kapaleeswarar temple in Mylapore (a renowned temple of Shiva located in Mylapore, Chennai, and moved to Sai Baba temple and prayed for a long time as advised by my father. At difficult times one doesn't dare disobey the advice to offer prayers at specific temples. Thereafter, I moved to CA Hanuman temple in Alwarpet. This Hanuman, according to many of my batchmates, including Anand, had the ability to help students become CAs and hence he was generally referred to as CA Hanuman. In my opinion, Anand must have garlanded this Hanuman at least six times with a vada mala (garland of vada) during his exam days. I was not sure if

I should have done this prior to the exams or prior to the results. I still went ahead with the principle of 'better late than never' and booked a 'vada mala' for the following Saturday irrespective of the fate of the result. Either it was thanksgiving or it was an advance booking for my next attempt. From Alwarpet, I went to the Shiva Vishnu temple in T. Nagar and all along the way I never failed to bow my head to every Ganesha or Durga or Amman temple I crossed. I could do it as I had chosen to walk rather than ride my old but reliable bike.

After the scheduled visits to the temples, I proceeded to Saravana Bhavan for their delicious breakfast. The hot filter coffee refreshed me.

Anand was expected home only at seven in the evening and our plan was to go the institute together. I was home by 12, and every minute seemed to be stretching interminably. Anxiety started to mount. I was sure that my BP reading would have also climbed up along with my heart rate, despite my young age. Perhaps, I thought optimistically, this was an indication that my career was likely to go up soon.

Anand came home on the dot and we left for the institute at around 10 pm, skipping dinner. He didn't seem to want any, or he perhaps had a different plan.

There was already a good crowd at the institute – the kind you can see when a Rajini movie is released. But here, no one was smiling. As if to test the candidates' forbearance, the results were published at around midnight as it had to come from Delhi.

The crowd grew larger in size and a mix of some bright, confident faces, anxious ones, and even some parents could be seen. There were people talking, praying, silently waiting… Many headed out to have tea and a smoke. The kirana shop made outside the institute was making additional business from the misery of many students.

At last the much awaited vehicle carrying the result papers entered the institute and candidates chased the car as if a celebrity was inside it, or as though it was an ambulance with a critically ill relative in it with minimal chances for survival. I had stopped chasing the car a year back.

The sheets that decided the fate of many students were getting pasted. I dreaded going near the notice board. Anand went instead as I waited near the gate, bogged down by anxiety and tension.

Five minutes... eight minutes... and finally twelve minutes later, Anand came running towards me, smiling gleefully. He hugged me, lifted me and said, "Congrats, Gautam, CA!" It took me a few seconds for this pleasant surprise to sink in. I hugged him tight and tears trickled down my cheeks. I now had the courage to go to the board and check the results. When we left the institute, it was around 12.15 am. A new day had dawned.

Anand and I partied till four in the morning. It was just us, and a bottle of rum and some beer. These bottles had been witnesses to my failure every six months. They deserved to be there as I celebrated my long-awaited success. We hit the bed at four in the morning and as a precaution to lessen the effect of hangover, we swallowed a Saridon each with three glasses of water before we dozed off. It was one of the best practices that one picks up in life.

ℓ

The Day after the Result

Anand didn't have the luxury of skipping office the next day. He was not at home when I woke up. There were a few messages in my phone. One message from an unknown number read – *"Congrats to the new CA, the new man in my life, love".*

I knew that was from Neha. I smiled as I texted my reply,

"thanks to the only woman in my life, from the same man with a better suffix now"

There was no reply to this message, and rightly so, as it was already 11 am, and unlike me, she would be battling some financial data at her workplace.

After fortifying myself with hot filter coffee, I spoke to my parents. They were extremely relieved and proud. Dad listed at least three or four corporate groups that I should consider (unmindful of whether they would consider me or not!) for seeking employment. He started with the Tatas and the Birlas and ended with the TVS group. After all, every parent wants his child to be well off. My reply that I would share with him my plans soon was met with silent disapproval. My unpreparedness within a day of passing didn't seem to impress him.

I distributed sweets in my office and was overwhelmed by the warmth with which my colleagues congratulated me. Even a couple of guys who had failed in their exams shared my success. I was blessed to have many well-wishers around me.

I informed my boss that I planned to quit in the next couple of weeks after handing over the accounts that I was handling. He kindly offered me a bigger role if I was interested, because of my customer management skills. Though touched by his warmth, I declined but promised to take his help with liberty whenever needed. Success changes the very air around the person. I left the office.

It was Friday and Anand would return from work at around eight. We normally dined in a good restaurant and then watched a movie in one of the best screens in the city – Satyam Complex. That day was going to be different though as Anand messaged me, saying, *"Hi, we are discussing something this night, be prepared, be relaxed... something very important."*

Only when you succeed, you have many options to choose

from. Till yesterday, I had only one subject to worry about; today I had to worry about too many things:

- What should I pursue?
- Dad's advice to join a reputed company.
- My boss' invitation to continue in the firm.
- Anand's message.
- My thanksgiving measure to CA Hanuman.
- Neha.

I decided that I would handle all of them professionally by prioritising. I was, after all, a qualified professional now!

Anand's plans were grand and it was two am by the time we wound up for the night.

♌

Venturing into a Venture

I felt I was not cut out to work in an organisation as an employee. Was it a reluctance to subject myself to serious interviews, facing the questions, the fear of rejection, or hesitation to compete with brighter and younger CAs. Whatever the reason, the prospect of an interview did not excite me. Partly this was a reason, yet, inside me, I could sense that I wanted to set up something of my own. Size didn't matter, there was no definition of success, and the urge to do something on my own was felt. I had dealt with some clients as an account head and had interacted with many unenthusiastic managing directors and CEOs of companies, had seen many unhappy faces at their work place purely because they were just going through the routine grind with the sole intention of earning their living. The excitement was missing. The place of work was without glitter and fun. I wanted to change this. I wanted to create an enterprise where I could see happy faces, a lot of fun, open interaction, no hierarchy based reservations to interact and, of course, a business model that worked and was sustainable. Again, success in financial terms was either taken for granted or completely ignored in my dream chase.

That left me with only one choice – to be on my own. My heart, rather than my head, dictated me to start something on my own. It was not just a desire. I was already asking myself, "What should I do to become an entrepreneur and what should the venture be?" I did not want to practice the profession. I was good at handling customers, so management consulting was one option. At the same time, it should be scalable, recurring and be needed by the whole universe. When you dream, dream big. I did. But I wasn't sure if I could do it alone. It is excellent and easy to dream alone. But when trying to make the dreams come true, you need someone with you, someone you trust.

Anand was curious to discuss my career plans and had done some homework on probable employers for me. There was also a requirement in his company, though he didn't want me to consider the same. I then shared my thoughts with Anand and narrated my plans of launching myself into self-employment!

"But why accounting services, Gautam?" Anand was puzzled that I was touching a subject that was relatively new at that point of time.

"Simple, Anand. Irrespective of the size of business, irrespective of the profitability of business and irrespective of the health of the economy, everyone needs accounting support. In fact, after tissue paper, the next most important service that would be perennially required by all is accounting and hence, accountants."

Anand laughed and hugged me. I thought he had mistaken my earnestness for a joke.

Launching myself into my own business with no business background and insufficient financial back-up was certainly risky, I was aware. If I didn't succeed commercially, I would not only lose my career but I also ran the risk of losing Neha forever, for no father would want his daughter to get married to someone who was struggling in his business or profession. I was evaluating the options, considering all relevant parameters. When I got up the next morning, Anand was not at home. He was not planning to go to work either, so I wondered where he was. I was having coffee when he returned. His forehead revealed that he had gone to some temple. On the way back, he had picked up hot idlis and vada from Sangeetha's.

"Anand, Neha hasn't called me yet, I am surprised," I said with concern.

"Oh man, I forgot to tell you. She is off-site somewhere and off communication. She will be back tomorrow." That reassured me

After breakfast and another round of hot coffee, Anand suddenly threw a question at me. "Gautam, what do you desire? To get a job or start something on your own?"

"I told you last night, I want to become an entrepreneur. That's where my heart and mind are," I replied promptly.

"Great, in that case I think we should get into accounting practice as it is a wonderful idea recommended by you."

"We meaning…?" I asked slowly, too excited to believe my ears.

"You and I," the reply was spot on.

"Are you joking?" I never thought that my qualifying could change his career path.

"I am quite serious about it," he said with a look that confirmed his words.

"Come on, you are in a stable job and doing well…" I played the devil's advocate.

"Quite true, Gautam. But I feel that if we have to take the risk, it is now or never."

"I admire your guts, man! You can afford to take the risk as you have industry experience and have saved some money in the last two years or so. Of course, you come from a bloody rich family too."

"Fuck! This attitude has to change. You have opened my eyes. I am also feeling sick of my job profile. I want to experiment the way you intend doing. Let's create something big, something we enjoy and something that is valuable and something that would be fulfilling." Anand spoke as though he had heard a motivational speech by one of the entrepreneurs who had a rags to riches story to tell. Yet, I could sense the truth in his statement, and more importantly, his conviction was abundant.

"But…I just qualified, and unlike you, I don't have practical accounting experience," I continued to punch holes, as much to convince myself as him.

"That's not a disadvantage. You don't have to worry about it as you don't have to dive deep into it. The best combo is that you handle marketing and business development and I handle operations. You have a natural talent there and you have the right look for business development. We are winning and winning together, and I hope you don't mind taking me as your partner in progress!" Anand was emphatic.

Honestly, he argued better than I could ever have. I had always trusted him and rejoiced that he considered me capable of being a worthy partner – someone responsible for revenues. The feeling was great.

I didn't say anything as my hug conveyed my happiness, my approval and my thanks.

"The money I have managed to save now can help me survive only for the next few months. After that, I will have to earn enough to pay my bills at least," I added one more caveat.

"No worries. If the situation arises, I shall help you. You don't need me to tell you that! From now on, we are not only good friends but also co-promoters," Anand reassured me, giving me a high-five.

"When do we sketch out our business plan?" My first positive statement since the discussion started made him look relieved.

"In the next fifteen days, buddy. I suggest that you travel to Bangalore and meet Neha. Then discuss your plans with your parents. Meanwhile, I shall resign as I need to give at least sixty days' notice," Anand summed up the plan of action.

Adrenaline rushed through my body. The prospect of meeting Neha as a qualified professional excited me. I wanted to assess her intentions towards me, and that added anxiety. I also had to convince my parents about my career choice. And then, I was to venture into a venture with my buddy. I couldn't have asked for anything more.

We went out for a beer lunch and said cheers to each other with a lot of cheer as we named our soon-to-be-launched business entity 'FAB SERVICES PVT LTD', with the tag line: 'We are accountable to you'. FAB was derived from the fact that it was a fabulous effort from two fabulous people to create a fabulous institution.

Brindavan Express to Bangalore

It was a Friday and a very convenient Brindavan Express was waiting for me, though I had reached the station well before time. I picked up a copy of *The Hindu* from Higginbotham's and started walking away. But I retraced my steps and picked up a copy of *The Economic Times.* Now that I was a qualified professional and, more importantly, someone who was already into a start-up, I was supposed to be reading all that hot and not hot stuff happening in the world of business.

The train was clean and I saw many happy faces among the passengers. Maybe they also had someone like Neha in their life waiting to receive them in Bangalore.

You never get bored travelling in the Brindavan Express, especially in the AC chair car. Plenty of eatables are sold one after another without even fifteen minutes' gap between each offering. From egg sandwiches to idli-vada-dosa, cutlet, poori masala – the list was close to infinite. In between, a few hundred litres of coffee, tea and coloured soft drinks are also offered.

Conversation hummed around me, but I didn't mind it as I was lucky not to be surrounded by noisy children. They create the maximum noise, empowered by health drinks such as Complan, Horlicks or Boost that keeps them awake during the entire journey.

I was also lucky to get a window seat. The man next to me was already day dreaming with his eyes closed and mouth open to allow at least two flies to enter simultaneously. Just across me sat a middle-aged lady and a very pretty girl in her twenties. The middle-aged lady was eager to pick up a conversation with me, I realized. I was pretending to read, not wanting to show how I was dying to talk to the girl.

"You must be a finance professional," was her first salvo.

For a moment I thought that she was addressing the day dreamer next to me, but if anything, his mouth was open a little wider.

"Yea, ma'am," I managed to reply as matter of factly as I could without looking at the younger girl too much and shut my mouth before the words 'at last' slipped out.

"I know, I guessed it right. You look like one! I could make out the way you were deeply engrossed in the share market page…"

I smiled and let her live in her delusion; how could I explain that this was the first time I had opened that page! I couldn't let my reputation suffer in front of a pretty girl.

"This is my daughter, Preeti."

"Hi Preeti, good to know you. I am Gautam," I said and shook her hands automatically, glad of the opportunity.

"Hello," she said smiling, looking even more beautiful. Seeing her tastefully worn short-sleeved black top with a snug fitting pair of tight jeans, and the shampooed, free flowing hair, I guessed she was either from Bangalore or had lived there a few years.

"So, you live in Bangalore," I continued the dialogue looking at Preeti but the reply came from her mom.

"Yea, we live in Bangalore. We had to attend a function in Chennai."

I was not interested in the mother and so hid behind *The Economic Times*, to impress the girl and to find something that I could understand.

There were several write-ups about and interviews with men in black suits and grey hair or no hair, on subjects ranging from managing fiscal deficits, curbing inflation, india outsourcing opportunities, to the RBI monetary policy, etc. There were also interviews with a few white-skinned people who expressed a lot of confidence in Indian markets and were very keen to explore the opportunities. I thought they were trying to jump into the quicksand without knowing it was one.

"Are you a CA?" Preeti's mom spoke again.

"Yea, I am." I consciously avoided the words 'at last' that were about to be uttered out of disclosure norms perhaps.

"I guessed so…you look like a CA. I can see it in your face," she was beaming with pride at her ability to guess aptly.

I hoped she was not trying to hook me up with her daughter. I wouldn't have minded had I not known of Neha's interest in me.

"Preeti has just joined CA and we are hoping that she would become a CA in her first attempt itself, maybe like you," she thought fit to add.

The law of probability never fails to prove its applicability. Her second guess was wrong, but for the sake of my reputation and image in front of a beautiful girl, I didn't want to prove her wrong.

"Yea, all that is required is focus and hard work," I replied looking at Preeti. She smiled and said that she could manage as she had always been a bright student. "Do you think I should refer to some specific books to improve my understanding of Costing?"

"Lots," I said sagely. "I recommend a few foreign authors' books."

The mere mention of 'foreign authors' made Preeti's mother widen her eyes, and my image improved instantly. She didn't know that I dreaded costing, and there was no reason for me to confess! After all, I was becoming an entrepreneur and the first lesson was not to reveal unnecessary information even to a stakeholder, leave alone an outsider.

After scanning a few more pages of *The Economic Times,* I shifted my focus to *The Hindu* and read a few film reviews, my favourite. Between articles on volatile crude prices and film reviews, the latter won hands down.

I realized that when I was scanning *The Economic Times,* Preeti had taken *The Hindu* paper from me (without my permission and without any annoyance on my part obviously) and had completed the crossword in less than thirty minutes. From then on, I was chatting with her mother with whom the conversation was easier and more comfortable.

Bangalore was just one hour away. I dozed off at some point reading the news about a golf tournament.

It was 1:15 pm when the train reached Bangalore Cantonment station, and I got down after exchanging many smiles with Preeti and her mother and after once again holding Preeti' hand for a while and wishing her success. Preeti's mother quietly handed over a piece of paper that had her mail id. "This is for you to mail the reference books for costing by foreign authors."The mail id read *'laksblore19@ yahoo.com'*.Women are too clever with regard to designing their email ids. Her name must have been Lakshmi, cut short to a trendy laks and 19 must have been her date of birth and clearly the year of birth never found its place in the id. I was a fool, my mail id was *'am_Gautam_1975@gmail.com.'* I immediately decided to change my mail id,for in the next fifteen years any stranger would know that I was forty years old. "Learn, entrepreneur, learn to maintain confidentiality," I told myself.

The First Date with Neha

I didn't know the way to the exit and decided to follow the herd heading in a particular direction – just as I had chosen CA. The difference was that in the case of the station, there would be an exit much sooner.

I had just made up my mind when someone tapped my shoulder. I turned around and was rendered speechless when I saw Neha standing there. My heart did all the talking.

"How are you Gautam? Congrats, you have won a long battle," she winked.

"Thanks Neha, it was a big relief. You know my dad well, and I am glad to escape his sarcasm about my capabilities."

"Were you surprised when Anand told you that I was waiting to see you?" her eyes twinkled.

"Of course, yes! Two great results at such short intervals… I hoped for both, but never imagined in my wildest dream that you'd have a special place for me in your heart," I replied bluntly.

Neha smiled, a nice mix of shyness and affection. "I want my life partner to be friendly, affectionate, smart, witty and enterprising…. I don't have to look far, do I?" My heart fluttered at having all these compliments showered on me at one go.

"There is something about you, man," Neha whispered softly, stepping closer, making me breathless.

Public display of affection is frowned upon in India, or else I would have clasped her to my bosom. But instead, I did the next best thing – played the sympathy card to strengthen her feelings for me.

"I can't believe it, Neha," I said with a genuine note of disbelief. "I thought you would seek a better match."

She laughed softly and said, "Come on dear…" As we walked with our hands grazing against each other, I could feel romance in the air.

"Tell me, Neha, why me? And why did you wait for so long?" My ego could do with some pampering!

"You never let on how you felt so I hesitated. But I could not forget you despite the distance and the time…"

I decided not to probe further, the same logic I applied when I cleared my CA final exams. Having passed, there was no need to probe about *how* one passed. Failure requires analysis but success doesn't. I cursed myself for my complex and the time we had wasted by being silent about our feelings. But not any longer. It was time to celebrate our mutually acknowledged feelings.

"I haven't had lunch," I informed. I was hungry as I hadn't eaten anything substantial in the train as I had preferred not to hog in the presence of a smart girl like Preeti. "Do you have to get back to work?"

"I have taken a day off. Let me take you to a nice place. My treat, being the earner here," she grinned and nudged my waist with her elbow.

"I know, you started earning while I was still yearning," I added with profound self-pity, which yielded better results as she put her slender arm on my shoulder and pulled me towards her, planting a kiss on my cheek.

Though the music began playing in the background, I was zapped. Neha had changed, to become the 'new normal', or better still, one of the 'bold and the beautiful' sort. Though she had also grown up in a conservative environment, one year in Bangalore had made her confident, bold and even smarter than she had been.

She was dressed immaculately in a pink shirt that had small white checks and had buttons where they were actually not required – on the pocket, at the end of the short sleeves, behind the collar and even below the collar; albeit the first button on the shirt was either missing or was stitched below the 'old normal' style. She was in a lovely pair of blue jeans that was hugging her slim long legs tightly. She had cut her hair and had a few strands of hair falling frequently on her forehead which she elegantly pushed back.

We hired an auto without the negotiation that one needed in Chennai and reached a place near Brigade Road. I had no luggage as I was returning the same night by the Chennai Mail. Neha paid the auto driver and I was surprised that the auto driver took the fare as per the meter. We entered a cozy restaurant and made ourselves comfortable on a corner table meant for two.

We ordered rotis, mattar paneer, and dal fry. I thought I would order some soup when Neha surprised me by asking if I wanted beer. My love for Bangalore – and Neha – was increasing by the minute.

"Wow, that would be great!" I said enthusiastically.

Cold beer replaced the hot soup but added more cheer to my first date with Neha. To my initial shock but growing excitement, Neha too got a mug for herself. We requested the waiter to serve the food a little later as we had ordered for two bottles of beer. We spoke of many things, we discussed many subjects, but what stands out in my memory is the way we held hands. We laughed a lot and the mood became more and more romantic as our eyes spoke of things our lips were yet too shy to say.

Neha worked for an IT company in the Finance & Accounting space (F&A). She was doing well and seemed to be extremely pleased with her employers.

I narrated my plans, the discussions with Anand, the launch of FAB Services and was gratified to hear Neha's enthusiastic approval.

"This is what you should be doing. I am thrilled, Gautam! You are entrepreneur material. Start early in business, build an enterprise. I have come across so many young entrepreneurs in Bangalore. I am sure there are great opportunities."

"Wow, I am so thrilled with your reaction. I have been dreading meeting my dad and convincing him about my decision to become an entrepreneur." I smiled at her and added, "Now I need to convince him about us as well! Not only my parents, but yours as well. Looks like my first sales pitch will be at home." We laughed out aloud.

"A good testing ground for your marketing skills! If you can't convince your own people, how are you going to convince your prospective clients?" Neha was talking like a manager now.

"I will do it. I have no choice as I am not going back on our collective dream of setting up the enterprise."

"You'll always have my support." She squeezed my hand warmly.

I grasped her hand with my free one, and this time, I had no intention of letting it go. Our eyes met and we fell silent, feeling the love between us.

"The topic of our love will have to wait," I said ruefully. "I don't think my dad can take two bullets at the same time." We chuckled, imagining my father fending off bullets coming from a gun in my hand.

"Take your time to settle down. I can wait. I am sure Anand and you will succeed soon," she reassured me, patting my hand.

"Yes, I am also confident. In the next three years, we should be able to build the company to a decent scale and when I am 28 or 29, we can get married." I was bluffing, of course. Though three years is a good long time to test ourselves in business, and many have succeeded in that much time, I was not so confident. Many factors contribute to success. They had to work for me too.

It was five when we left the restaurant. She was visibly happy. We had four hours or so before my train's scheduled departure. We walked through the streets, our hands clasped, our shoulders touching. The weather outside and the mood in our hearts was just right. On Neha's suggestion, we went to her small one bed room apartment in Malleshwaram that she shared with her colleague from the same company. It was well maintained and comfortable.

The apartment had all the required gadgets – TV, fridge, coffee maker, bread toaster, washing machine and a decent music system. An air conditioner was missing, but Bangalore weather didn't need one for most months in the year.

As I refreshed myself, I realized that I was feeling at home. Neha made some coffee and we chatted undisturbed!

As the evening lights came on and the mood mellowed, I inched closer and wrapped my arms around her. She nuzzled against me, and it was as if we were long lost lovers meeting unexpectedly. I kissed her tentatively on her lips, and then as she reciprocated, we drifted away from this world. It was fabulous despite the Kingfisher flavour. Even when we finally separated, we remained silent. We didn't need any words.

I left her apartment reluctantly at seven and Neha came to the station to see me off. Before I got into the train, we hugged and she whispered in my ears shyly, "In kissing, you have cleared the exam in the first attempt!" I laughed to cover up my embarrassment! I hated having to leave her.

I hung from the stairs of my compartment waving to Neha, who walked with the train till she could keep up no more. Even after the speck of Neha vanished, I hung on to the memory and the handle bar. I finally tore myself and headed to my berth carrying lots of good memories, excitement and some ounces of tension. I hit the berth and slept deeply and peacefully till I reached Chennai.

ᔕ

Things to do – Prelude to the Business Plan

The Bangalore trip gave me the confidence that even if it took a few more years than the 'old normal' in business, I would 'settle down in personal life' sooner or later – that is, getting married and start a family.

I gave Anand a heavily censored version of my Bangalore trip, but he filled up the gaps himself and was genuinely excited at our plans to marry in the near future. He also felt pleased that Neha supported the idea of our new venture, my becoming an entrepreneur and partnering with Anand.

Celebrations over, Anand and I sat down for a serious discussion on Wednesday evening.

I took a piece of paper and wrote with a lot of pride:

'FAB MANAGEMENT SERVICES INDIA PVT LTD founded by Anand Palaniappan and Gautam Vaidyanathan.'

Anand graciously modified it marginally as founded by Gautam Vaidyanathan and Anand Palaniappan. He explained that since it had been my idea originally, this was the right order. I punched him affectionately on his gradually growing paunch.

The next few 'things to do' were jotted down quickly. Of course, later in our business journey, we would realize that it was always easier to list down 'things to do' than actually see them moving to 'things done' list. I specialized in making the 'to do list' while Anand was responsible for the execution.

The list was grouped under the following simple heads –

WHAT
WHEN
WHERE
HOW

WHY was consciously avoided as there was no question of WHY; we had burnt the boats after reaching the shore and there was no ambiguity at least on WHY. Over an interactive chat between the new founders, we completed the four headings with a few more bullet points under them –

WHAT: types of service offerings under Accounting.
WHEN: March 2003
WHERE: ??? a reasonably prime business address.
HOW: ???

Not a bad beginning! We congratulated ourselves on the first informal board meeting of the company under formation. In fact, it was such mutual appreciation even for simple, silly tasks that drove, propelled, ignited and motivated us to build a corporate entity with no real support, background and legacy.

Since we were extremely tired after our first board meeting (!), we settled for a very small drink to celebrate our first Macro Business Plan. We had ordered food from a Chinese joint and had our first business dinner that night.

It was perhaps around 1.30 am when I suddenly woke up, groped in the dark a bit and managed to reach my desk without disturbing Anand. I pulled out the business plan sheet and went to the other room. The next one hour, I thought through the simple tasks that needed to be attended in some order and used a second sheet to add bullet points to what we had jotted down earlier.

WHAT:
Accounting–end to end accounting, AP Processing, AR Management, Financial Accounting system consulting, Reconciliation Activities, Management Accounting, MIS, etc.

WHEN:
23 March 2003. For some unfathomable reason, I have an affinity to the number 5, be it 5, 14 or 23. For me, 5 is a mercurial number. Need I point out that it took me five attempts to clear my CA exams?

WHERE:
Nungambakkam, Alwarpet or Mylapore – preferably Dr. Radhakrishnan Road if we decide on Mylapore.

HOW:

- Get company incorporated soon and ensure we get the name we want (unless another company with a similar name existed, I think this will be a cakewalk).
- Build a small paid-up capital to fund the set-up cost and the working capital, at least for the first six months to one year. Main contribution to come from Anand as he is earning a reasonable salary and comes from a fairly well to do family.
- Hire people, at least the skeleton staff.
- Create marketing collaterals and hire inexpensive brand consulting guys to create logos and other corporate communication aids.
- Device the 'go-to-market' strategy, list the names we know, our network, explore the network of the network and anyone who could give us some break, some tasks and, more importantly, some hope.

'Go FORWARD and STRICTLY NO LOOKING BACK' – I wrote in bold so that even in difficult times, we would never give up hope. *I firmly believe that anyone who wants to set up any enterprise should write this statement in bold letters, directly proportional to the size of their fear and indecisiveness.*

I also wrote separately two other important 'things to do':

- Anand to get the relieving order before 28 February 2003.
- Visit Pondicherry to shock my parents, especially my dad, with my decision to start a venture, and to ensure that even if he did not bless me, at least he would not curse me!

I was glad at my handiwork and finally returned to bed an hour later.

♌

Pondicherry – The first trip after becoming a qualified CA

Anand, who was getting relieved from his job in three weeks, planned to pitch for some accounting work from his current employer. It would be a small beginning, and would still add a lot of value to our profile. I could also get some references from my boss as there would be no conflict of interest. However, the only risk was that he still offered me a larger role in his firm and had even tried to dangle the carrot of partnership at some point of time, may be on his death bed. So I carefully planned how I would word my request and my impending resignation. I feel proud even today that I did so without burning the bridges.

I picked up some devotional sweets from Grand Sweets, Adyar; devotional because I was given a few free sloka books as freebies since I had made a purchase for a considerable amount. This long-time practice of Grand Sweets to add value to its customers was a lesson I imbibed once our business flourished. I also had my quota of free sweet pongal and then headed for Nalli's in T. Nagar to buy a sari for my mom and a shirt for my dad. I removed the price tag since I knew my dad would definitely look at it and curse the businessmen for fleecing their customers. This boded badly for me because soon, I would also belong to the same class and become the subject to his displeasure…once again!

Instead of travelling by bus as usual, I hired a taxi near Meenambakkam airport. The taxi had brought a passenger from Pondicherry to Chennai airport and was returning empty. Normally such drivers scout for such customers as they make some money, and for the customers, the fare would definitely be reasonable – a clear win-win deal for the driver and the passenger, though it was a clear financial loss for the owner. I was happy with the elevation from a bus to an air-conditioned taxi, or rather, a car.

When the taxi reached my home, my mother came out smiling proudly at the fact that her qualified and eligible son had engaged a car. To her it was a sign of prosperity and pride She herself had never seen such luxuries because of my father's parsimony.

My dad was reading *The Indian Express* when I entered the house. He congratulated me whole-heartedly, adding that all his prayers ultimately yielded results. I was tempted to ask if on the earlier occasions, he hadn't prayed properly or did so to the wrong god? I swallowed the thought because I needed to keep his ego massaged and him in good spirits.

He wondered if the car was provided as a perk by my prospective employer. He imagined that I had either joined a TVS group company or a Cholamandalam group company. He had fixed deposits in both these companies and perhaps hoped that my induction into either of these groups would further secure his deposits! I diplomatically left that question unanswered and instead handed the sari and the sweets and snacks to my mother and the shirt to my dad. My mother was delighted with the bright looking poly cotton sari with zari that I had picked for her. My dad did the Google search – he put on his reading glasses to look for the price on the sari and his shirt. Not finding the tag, he asked me the price, but I remained mum. It was similar to the 'compulsory question' that I had faced several times in my exams and many a time I had ignored replying to them. Frustrated with my silence, he made a wild guess and quoted a price that was just half what I had paid. I let him believe that, as even at that price, he thought I had been naive.

The home was filled with the amazing aroma of my mother's cooking. The aroma was a jugalbandi of rava kesari, poori masala, bisibella bath and freshly fried pappads.

After a sumptuous lunch, I slept like a python; nothing could disturb me for three hours. When I woke up, it was almost five pm, there were a few visitors at home. I joined the two uncles, two aunties, four school going children and one very old lady after freshening up. There was that usual question one had to face several times, especially during weddings. Middle-aged and old people derive pleasure in embarrassing the young ones by asking, "Do you know me? Tell me my name." One of the elders decided to test my knowledge and I nodded, and was glad that they did not probe further to test my memory.

There were plenty of wishes and advice about what I should do next. Someone opined that CAs were in great demand in the marriage market, making my mother grin from ear to ear.

After they finally left, I shot the first bullet – that I was setting up my business!

"We are from a normal middle class family, this will not suit us," my dad reacted along expected lines.

"Dad, if we were from a million dollar family, I would have gone for employment as there would be no further need to create wealth," I retorted. My mom was silent, unable to take sides. Perhaps she wondered if she would be denied of a sari if I didn't start earning right from day one.

The debate was spiced with cynical remarks and dire warnings. When I remained bull-headed, my dad washed his hands off summarily, "It is your life, you do what you want to. But remember, no one from our community will be willing to give his girl in marriage to you unless you earn well."

"That's fine, dad. I don't care if I don't get married," I replied arrogantly, confident on that count, but unwilling to bring up Neha's name just then. After all, there will be plenty of opportunities to rake it up later. The only saving grace was that I was partnering with Anand, whom they liked and thought of as serious. According to them, only serious people succeeded in professional life.

By the time I left Pondicherry two days later, my dad had come around and even offered to lend me money if I needed any. I knew that he had to break a few fixed deposits in case I opted for such help from him. My eyes dimmed with tears and I thanked God for giving me such a wonderful dad. His blessings boosted my confidence and increased my sense of responsibility.

March 2003

Leasing a Property for Office

I took up the responsibility of identifying the office space as I had all the time in the world. The easiest source was *The Hindu* rental classified space. I jotted down as many as fifteen numbers with four things in mind –

- The office space should be anywhere between 1000 and 1200 square feet though initially only three would occupy it – me, Anand and an office assistant. An office assistant would be needed to get tea and coffee when the directors of the company were stressed out because of the pressure of the business. Or rather, the pressure to get the business!
- No brokers! Of course, we didn't have the budget to pay brokers.
- Should be anywhere between Nungambakkam and Mylapore.
- Furnished, to safeguard our cash outflows.

From the fifteen, I shortlisted the following names as they sounded cool –

- Ms Rashmi Agarwal – sounded stylish and I was intrigued. Just basic instinct.

- Mr. Vijayaraghavan – sounded easy to deal with.
- Mr. Seshadri – perhaps an old man who wouldn't be greedy.
- Goodwill Poor Children Uplift Trust – obviously a charitable trust and I trusted that the rental expectation would be low!

My first meeting was with Rashmi Agarwal. She lived in a posh bungalow. I was stopped by the security guard at the gate. And on hearing voices, a very well built German Shepherd came running to the gate, barking menacingly.

I explained the reason for my visit in my highly broken Hindi – thanks to Big B, SRK, Amir Khan, Salman Khan and the like, whose movies I watched despite the language divide. I understood their stories better than SADP (Systems Analysis and Data Processing) in the CA finals. I was allowed inside after the barking dog, which didn't seem to believe in 'barking dogs seldom bite', was tied in one corner. This German Shepherd's anger was further aggravated at being kept at bay and I could hear him roaring even after I had entered the house.

I waited in the sit-out, reading a *Stardust* kept handily to update myself about who-is-going-with-whom, when the landlady Rashmi Agarwal came out. Probably in her late thirties, she was slightly fat but attractive. Many South Indian men desire slightly fat ladies, whom we euphemistically refer to as 'healthy' ladies. A few coloured strands of hair fell elegantly on her forehead. Her smooth neck was adorned by a beautiful little diamond chain, and she wore glittering bangles. Her branded footwear lifted her height by at least four inches. She was in a bright, well-ironed sari and a stylishly cut blouse. The trip seemed well worth it.

I introduced myself and assured her of safety of the property and prompt payment of the rent. She had a property in Nungambakkam in one of the prominent commercial complexes. For a space of 1400 sq ft, she expected a rent of Rs 24,000 and a minimum of eight months' advance. It was not furnished and was just a shell space. I tried hard to negotiate, but in vain. Finally I told her that 1400 sq ft was a little too big for us and we would settle for something in the range of 1000 sq ft. As she had nothing more to offer, our conversation came to an end and I was blessed with a view of her expansive back. As I left, the dog seemed to sense his mistress' disappointing meeting and started to bark again. I knew I wouldn't have succeeded in negotiating the rent and opted not to feel disappointed with my negotiation skills knowing very well what her expectations were.

My next stop was Alwarpet, where Mr. Vijayaraghavan lived. It was a posh location and definitely a good address for office or residence. As against Rashmi, who was in a fashionable chic blouse, Mr. Vijayaraghavan was absolutely shirtless! His protruding belly and inches of flesh oozing around his waist line indicated that he had not moved a muscle for several years. His house was messier than a shabbily maintained room of a hostel boy. A strange odour from the drawing room added to the gloom.

He offered his 1100 sq ft space on the first floor at just Rs 7,500 as he was very keen to let out his property to a CA professional, he claimed. Though the rent was very attractive, the property and the owner were not. I escaped quickly saying I would discuss the matter with my partner before confirming.

After a quick bite in a hotel nearby, I reached the office of Goodwill Poor Children Uplift Trust in one of the lanes of T. Nagar. As the place was in a dingy lane, it took me a while to find it.

From the moment I entered the office, I found it a bit eerie. The lady at the desk constantly smiled at me for no reason as I waited, making me wonder if I should have also reciprocated with a smile but fear and uneasiness over powered diplomacy. She introduced herself as Pallavi and smiled again. She looked like a B grade movie actress without proper make-up. Within a few minutes, another fat, dark lady walked in. She smiled even more broadly and sat very close to me. She introduced herself as Sarala and told me that the trust owned the property measuring 2200 sq ft and that they would give 1000 sq ft to a tenant for commercial purpose – the words 'commercial purpose' seemed to have a different meaning! Again a smile from Sarala! I was dead sure that this was not a trust in the real sense and that instead of uplifting the lot of poor children, they were into child trafficking. I escaped after being bestowed a smile once again by the two ladies.

I was disappointed, to say the least. Three prospective landlords and none satisfactory. From Rashmi Agarwal to the paunchy, shirtless Vijayaraghavan to the suspicious Pallavi and Sarala, the class of prospective landlords was sliding, and sliding very badly.

My last chance was with Mr. Seshadri at Mylapore. He lived in a nice modern apartment near Vivekananda College. He greeted me warmly. I gave him my background and the details of the new business venture plans and assured him of our commitment to pay rent promptly. All he said in reply was that he was comfortable with me as I was a South Indian Brahmin (Iyer). I mentally thanked my parents! Mr. Seshadri had a blind faith on my values and commitment. In the meantime, a middle-aged lady (mami), most probably his wife, brought some hot filter coffee for me. The coffee was excellent and if accompanied by onion pakodas, would have completed the delicious serving. The mami had very good aura about her.

The property was at Dr Radhakrishnan Road, 1400 sq ft in area, reasonably furnished. The very nice mama offered it for just Rs 12,200 per month, and an advance for just five months.

He even showed some photographs taken inside the office including a couple of pictures taken from outside. The elevation looked quite impressive. The office space looked neat and spacious. There were even a few work stations good enough for fifteen people and that minimized the need for us to spend enormous amount of money in building work stations. I used his good nature for our benefit and requested him to freeze the rent for two years, twenty-two months to be precise and lease deeds were to be entered every eleven months.

I didn't even opt to see the place prior to my acceptance. I knew that we wouldn't get a better place at such a rate and at such terms. For a start-up firm, getting a good office space at the right address and terms was a boon. I prostrated before him and requested his good wishes and blessings. He was visibly moved. I assured him that we would sign the lease deed in the next five days and occupy the place on 23 March. Before I left the house, I saw a photograph of a beautiful girl between mama and mami. He told me that she was his daughter, a brilliant student, an acclaimed Carnatic singer, a budding Bharathanatyam artiste and an impeccable chef in the kitchen. Mami's eyes glowed with pride. I smiled and left the place, realizing that Mr. Seshadri was perhaps too kind to me as he had his own calculations in mind. As nothing obvious was indicated, I felt no guilt about not mentioning my being committed.

As I climbed down the stairs at 5 pm, I recapped all that had happened.....

Space of 1400 sq ft
Rent of Rs 12,200
Lease deed within 5 days
Rent advance 5 months
Occupation from 23 March

Wow, the magic of the number '5' continued! I knew we were on track.

I went back home happy, excited and wiser. The taste of filter coffee still lingered favourably on my tongue.

ℓ

The Inauguration and the Initial Set-up

There were just a few days to go for the soft launch of our company. Starting from getting the approval of the name of the company to furnishing the office (!), getting the people, signing a few clients and creating a profit & loss account and a balance sheet, there was so much waiting for us. Even today, Anand and I recall those fantastic days, perhaps the most exciting days of our business. The first five years...when we didn't build the business brick by brick, but grain by grain.

We made a ball park calculation on the working capital requirement and the initial capital expenditure including rent advance. We were prudent in our estimates and resolved to provide for one year! The objective was to enable us to focus on building the business without breaking our head in meeting our monthly overheads at least for a specific period of time. The total summed up to Rs 10 lakhs – we had factored in rent, salaries for a couple of resources, power, travel and conveyance, communication costs and other miscellaneous expenses apart from cash outflow towards rent advance, office furniture and computers. I just had one lakh and Anand managed to bring in seven lakhs. We still had a deficit of two lakhs, but that's the way one sets up a business. You are never in an ideal situation that would make you idle!

We chose three names to apply to the Registrar of Companies (ROC) in Form 1A-

- FAB Management Services India P Ltd
- FAB Management Services P Ltd
- FAB Consulting P Ltd

We debated if our entity could be a partnership firm instead of a private limited company to avoid the complexity and formalities not only in creation and running, but in winding up of the business in case such a situation arose. Yet, running the business under a corporate banner always creates a better perception. And, very often, perseverance and perspiration have to be supported by perception to achieve the desired results. I call them the 3Ps of success.

To save time, we prepared the Memorandum and Articles of Association of the company (draft copy) with the help of a practicing company secretary. We had to fill up the name of the company after getting the approval from ROC. Anand was magnanimous enough to insist that we have an equal stake in the company despite his initial investment being far higher than mine. My pleas for him to take a higher stake for himself fell onto deaf ears. Just to convince me, he finally agreed to take the money with interest from me the day we sold the company. Though I knew he was giving in only in appearance, I had to yield to his very kind gesture flowing from his golden heart. I thought to myself that the first step for any success was the right association and right intention. I couldn't have asked for anything more then. It was a very proud moment for us to fill a few details in the Memorandum of Association including an Authorized Capital of Rs 25 lakhs when all that I had in my bank account was Rs 30,000 after allocating one lakh towards my initial investment into our new company. That's the thrill in entrepreneurship – trying to create something out of nothing or many things out of something. Such a kick in life can never be measured in monetary terms even by any of the well-calibrated measuring instruments.

We decided to invite a few of our well-wishers and friends for the launch of the company. The list included my ex-boss, a few of Anand's colleagues including some of his seniors in the company he worked and a few friends who would play a pivotal role in getting us free visibility and marketing. We included our parents too in the invitees' list as we wanted to send them a clear message that we were getting into serious business, or rather into business, seriously. I did not want to include Neha at this stage as I did not want to send any signals to my parents at the wrong time.

Eventually the list totaled to almost twenty. We personally invited most of them. When I went to invite my ex-boss, I massaged his ego carefully so that he was eager to introduce me to some of his clients. Anand followed a similar course of action in his former company. These references and the consequent business deals helped us earn revenues in the initial days without having to provide for bad debts.

The launch was on 5 April though the lease deed was effective from 23 March. Anand and I shopped for office furniture, basic stationery, window blinds, etc. It was an exciting experience that that later came in handy when setting up our homes after our respective marriages. Only, in this case, there was no pressure from our better halves. Anand left the choice to me, giving me complete freedom.

We had planned to buy one desktop computer, one laptop, but had to settle for only one due to our financial crunch. An air conditioner for our cabin, on the other hand, was a must in Chennai. Since we shared a cabin, one AC was enough. In fact, after the business grew multi-fold, we continued to share the cabin. Such was our comfort level.

In the meantime, we successfully incorporated our company and FAB Consulting Pvt Ltd was born. We now had no option but to run and grow this company since winding up was a greater challenge; this was something I didn't STUDY properly while I was a student but something I READ very carefully before setting up a company. The name cards were printed with a logo created by a friend whose hobby was creating logo designs. We got that for free. Our company name read-

FAB Consulting Pvt Ltd

count on us

I chose the tag line 'count on us', which was instantly approved by Anand. Neha too, who messaged to say, *'count on me as well'*. Though we managed to get only the third name option in our application with ROC, we were in reality excited because 'consulting' always has a perceived value and added sophistication to even the ordinary services that one may render.

I had originally thought of 'we are accountable' but then realized that such a tag line would encourage the clients to increase the penalty clauses in the contracts.

We arranged for Ganapathy homam on 5 April, followed by breakfast from Saravana Bhavan and a simple memento for each guest. Though more people turned up that day, it was well within our budget. My boss brought a couple of his clients and the crowd from Anand's earlier company was a bit more than was anticipated. If anything, this assured us of our success as we had well-wishers from day one! And it all started on 5 April, 5 being a mercurial number to me.

Our landlord was also invited and he was also extremely elated. I am sure he would have felt relief that he would get his rent on time looking at the way we had launched our office religiously! And sincerely as well. He was also a witness to the several words of appreciation that my ex-boss uttered at good decibel levels with a purpose; he was very kind to me.

My boss took me aside and gave me one piece of advice, "Gautam, congrats on setting up a corporate entity. You may need a smart guy from a business school since, as accountants, we may lack the necessary glamour needed for marketing and even for strategic reasons. You need to get someone to fill the gap. If not now, as you move forward, this may be important to your company. Keep this in mind. I know, it would cost a lot to engage someone from a business school as an employee but there could be other ways of engaging one….think!"

After everyone left, Anand and I shook hands. Our smiles turned to happy laughter. We looked forward to a life of excitement, purpose, anticipation and fear.

Out of the total estimated 'office launch' expenses, we were left with Rs 400. We picked up a few chilled beer bottles, some snacks and packed some food on our way back home in Anand's new addition to his life–a brand new Hero Honda bike.

ᔓ

FAB – First Three Mandates

Anand and I decided that we wouldn't draw any salary during the first year of operation and dreamt of meeting our expenses with the revenues we generated.

The first three assignments came through references, not very interesting ones, yet something to make us get up in the morning with hope. We had in the meantime recruited an office assistant and a basic accountant. The first two were through my ex-bosses. The first one, a paint company, had huge issues of reconciliation of dealer and vendor accounts which it had neglected the past few years. Now the parent company in the US had warned the Indian company to set things right within a prescribed timeline. Since they did not have enough resources, they decided to hire an external agency for reconciliation. It was an opportunity for us since we would be engaged for at least six months. Anand also managed to get an assignment relating to Fixed Assets Accounting, creation and maintenance of the FA Register. This involved offsite work as well as onsite for seeking clarification and verification of invoices, etc. To manage both these assignments simultaneously, we had to get another accounting assistant on a temporary basis from a firm known to us.

The miracle was that FAB made marginal profits within the first four months, without taking into account the promoter directors' salaries. Soon we realized that we were on track... on the fast track. The billing crossed Rs 1 lakh within the first three months.

We grasped the importance of cash flows and we even developed some financial discipline in our personal life. The several phone calls I used to make to Neha got partly replaced by messaging.

On a Monday morning, I got a call from Neha, "Hi Gautam, how are you? I hope I am not disturbing you if you're in a conference call or a meeting?" she giggled.

"Teasing me? Watch it, Neha, in the next three years I may have to miss many of your calls due to my busy schedule and business priorities!" It was my turn to give it back to her.

"Sorry man, in that case, you may have to miss me altogether." Neha put me in a fix.

"Oh in that case, I take back my statement!" I replied, chastised. Little did I realize that even in later part of my life, I would answer calls from my wife Neha despite being in the midst of a meeting. Her early warning did the trick, and I enjoyed giving in to her demands.

"I have some good news, and bad news," Neha continued. "Which one do you want to know first?"

"Obviously, the bad news. I am used to hearing the bad news first before I get any good news," I replied with false bravado. Was she getting engaged to someone else because of pressure from her parents? Should I then be forced to consider the back-up at a later date? The picture of my landlord's daughter flashed in my mind.

"Okay, the bad news is that I am off to the US for the next two years and the good news is that I have been promoted, I have moved up in grade."

I didn't answer immediately, caught between a sense of emptiness and elation on her behalf. "Great, Neha! I am not surprised about your promotion. I am sure the US stint will be great for your growth!"

"Yea, I hope so, Gautam. But I will miss you a lot, so you better make sure you chat with me regularly!"

"Of course, I will miss you too. When are you leaving?"

"In the next twenty days. I already have a valid visa. I will give you more details later this evening as I need to go for a meeting now."

The call ended, but left me with a lot of thoughts, mostly good in a way. I knew I would be missing Neha, but was happy that she had gotten this opportunity. Even the bad news turned out to be good in a way, as I was able to focus fully on building my business. I had set a stiff target for FAB that couldn't brook distractions. I had not even shared it with Anand – a billing of Rs 12 lakhs by the financial year-end, meaning another Rs 10 lakhs plus in the next nine months.

We achieved a turnover of Rs 9.50 lakhs in the first year and started drawing our first salary from January – a small but an important beginning.

December 2005

The Business grows and Anand gets Engaged!

In the first two to three years of entrepreneurship, Anand and I realized that the main formula for growth was tolerance and sustenance, accompanied by some smart, instant and even impulsive decisions. And, more than anything else, placing the company's interests above our personal interests. In the long run, this resolution aided by our attitude towards work and life took this company to great heights.

FAB had become a 20-people company and the team consisted of resources (the new vocabulary for 'people') with different skill sets, qualifications and packages. Revenues were moving up and so were the number of clients. Although we were pitching for core accounting services, we were mostly getting allied activities that were comfortably packaged under 'accounting' for the purpose of our pitch. A few small and medium sized companies mandated us to set up accounting system and processes, including reporting. Wherever possible, we retained the 'reporting' function as an outsourced, high end service.

To secure decent working capital, we kept our salary low, but it had grown from what we had started with. We were disciplined about the following -

- Pay rent on time.
- Pay salary on the third day of every month.

- Pay all other bills one or two days before the due date.
- Draw our salary in two instalments.
- Never bribe anyone to get business.

In the first two years, we focused on getting business from Chennai-based companies. We networked with as many people as possible and kept ourselves abreast with the developments in the world of commerce, relevant to our business.

Out of the twenty people on the rolls, almost ten were deployed at client locations. We did not project ourselves or even desire to be a 'staffing solutions' company – we just marginally modified our business model as an on-site and off-site Accounting Services company. One of the ways to assess the growth of an entity is to evaluate the additional slides in one's presentation deck periodically, particularly if there are some additions to new services, new credentials, better infrastructure, etc. We could see that happening to our own entity.

Neha had returned from the USA a couple of months back and she had even mailed a few pictures taken there. She seemed to have become more beautiful, thanks to the better living conditions and the weather in the US. Her confidence had also grown big time. At least two or three times, she had mentioned over phone that we were in the right line of business and that she felt that one day FAB would handle services for clients in America too. I dismissed it as fantasy since our business had not even crossed the borders of Chennai. We met during some weekends, and I hoped for clientele in Bangalore so that I would have more reasons to visit her on weekdays as well. She was not keen to work in Chennai as she had totally fallen in love with Bangalore unsurprisingly.

One Sunday morning, Anand got a call from his father. After that, he seemed disturbed. There were no secrets between Anand

and me, and he confessed that his bad mood was because of a marriage proposal. There was a lot of emotional pressure from his parents since Anand could be a rebel when he felt like.

"It is bugging, man! I can easily wait for two more years to get married," he fumed.

"Explain that to your parents, be adamant," I suggested, placing my hand gently on his shoulder. Many men dread getting married and very rarely have I have seen a man smiling when he announces his impending wedding. The pressure always seems to overshadow the pleasure.

"No chance! My mother is shedding copious tears. Can't handle so much emotional blackmail. Her mother is 75 years old and that old lady wants to screw up my happiness before she hits the grave. If she wants to see some function at home, she could get married now to another sick man. I can't understand this nonsense," he raved and ranted, making me laugh uncontrollably.

With the maternal grandmother pressurizing through the mother, there was little the father or son could do. The only way forward was to yield to the pressure and become a slave to the situation.

"Who is the lucky girl?" I realized that Anand was coming to terms with the reality just the way we agree to pricing with most of our clients.

"Someone distantly related. She is not exposed to urban living or thinking, I guess. My mom says she is a sweet looking girl and knows our culture well."

I never understood what 'culture' had to do with marriage. If there is some pathology lab that specializes in such 'culture tests', I am sure it will give them humungous business.

"Advance congratulations, my friend," I genuinely consoled, sorry, congratulated him.

"The girl is going to be in Chennai for a day or two to attend a wedding. My parents are also coming here at the time and we will be meeting her and her parents. If things go well, I am finished... I mean, I will be engaged to her," he said and then looked at me beseechingly. "You have to come with me."

I agreed, hoping for some fun.

Before his parents' visit to our apartment, we cleared up the place and threw out all the empty liquor bottles; surprisingly, there weren't that many.

On Friday morning, Anand's parents landed at our apartment with the seventy-five-year-old granny who seemed to still dominate the proceedings at home. She was quite healthy, and would keep her grave waiting. Anand's father, while thanking me for convincing his son to agree to getting engaged, also advised me to 'settle down' soon. I merely smiled.

Soon everybody reassembled in the drawing room. Anand was in a new, formal shirt and trousers. The seventy-five-year-old was in a sparkling green silk sari, the size of the border reflecting her wealth and affluence. Her nose ring and earrings, both diamonds, sparked against her dark skin that she had tried to cover with an extra layer of talcum powder.

On the way to the venue, Anand's father told me that the girl's father had promised an apartment for his daughter after the wedding as dowry so that they young couple could live happily ever after! I had been wondering what would happen to our flat once Anand brought his wife, and was relieved to hear of this development. Of course, the burden of the rent would fall on me now.

The 'meeting' was planned at The Residency in T. Nagar. We had hired a Honda City as Anand's granny wanted to flaunt their affluence and Anand's dad willingly yielded. We reached the lobby of the hotel and met a welcoming committee of at least nine people from the girl's side. Anand was in great demand! The girl's father welcomed each of us warmly with folded hands, a part of culture that Anand should soon pick up or would be forced to pick up. When I was introduced to them, I conveyed my apologies for being an unwelcome guest (most of the time, I get this feeling of being unwelcome when I go for sales pitch with disinterested yet prospective clients).

"Any friend of Anand's is most welcome," the man said drawing from his unending source of warmth.

I spotted the prospective one by the way she was dressed. She was short, fair – an edge in any marriage deal – and definitely had poor dressing sense. The jasmine flowers in her hair overpowered the smell of the room freshener in the lobby. She seemed fearless and dominating, I laughed to myself as I thought of the poor grandmother whose position seemed threatened.

Finding an opportune moment, Anand took me aside and asked me eagerly, "What's your opinion, be frank da." He didn't seem aware that even his own opinion was immaterial, let alone mine.

"Talk to her first," I replied diplomatically.

As we entered the lobby again, we saw the girl prostrating despite it being a public space. The seventy-five-year-old, her ego massaged, immediately announced that the girl would be their daughter-in-law and that Anand would only be too pleased to accept her decision. My friend's smile was forced, just as we put on a fake smile when signing up and shaking hands with our clients when we enter into a new contract at ridiculous rates and with terms and conditions completely in favour of the clients.

The feasting stretched over two hours to celebrate this announcement. Anand's father-in-law was proud that his son-in-law was on his own, unlike my father who though supportive on the surface, seemed to be waiting for my fall. Anand spoke to the girl, Divyalakshmi, and introduced her to me as 'Divya' though the others called her Lakshmi.

After lunch, the meeting came to an end. The wedding was scheduled to be held in the next four to six months. Anand's family left for Madurai that night and we celebrated Anand's informal engagement (as a formal engagement was held a few days later at Anand's place) with a beer each. It marked the re-entry of the empty bottles at home!

June 2006

Red Sand Funds, BKC Complex, Mumbai

This was the time many PE (Private Equity) firms and Venture Capital Funds (VCs) were entering India. India was clearly on the radar for investments for some of these firms who were willing to take a long term strategic bet on the Indian economy, especially the IT and BPO companies. When you don't gain in the short term, you always adopt a long-term strategy. The concept of angel investors, VCs and PEs was relatively new to many Indian entrepreneurs. Though some investments were happening from the above three categories of investors, most of them were made in IT and BPO companies. The BPO industry was growing at an enviable rate in India. The youth was working on graveyard shifts, helping people in the US fix their problems such as a computer not booting up, microwave not working or resolving their queries about their credit cards. Many call centres had been set up in India. It was a time when the Murugans were becoming Morgans and Selvis were becoming Stellas. The good side to it was that many who would have continued to remain roadside Romeos or just hang around the bourgeoning malls were getting employed.

Red Sand Funds had just set up an office in India a few months back. They were at the top most floor in one of the tallest glass buildings in BKC, Mumbai, no doubt saying things like: "We have to be on top and have a bird's view of the economy." Red Sand had built a strong team in India under the stewardship of Jayant Mathur, the CEO, who suited the role perfectly.

It was an important day at Red Sand as Jayant was to address the entire team. An alumnus of IIT Mumbai and IIM Ahmedabad, he also had a doctorate in Economics from Stanford USA. He was in his early 40s, but being a fitness freak and an active golfer who was frequently seen on Page 3, he didn't look a day over 30. He had very good work experience and exposure in the Banking and Financial Services industry, especially in the lucrative Investment Banking segment. He also had a great understanding of Indian business, economy, entrepreneurship spirit, culture, diversity and, more importantly, the challenges, lack of governance, poor infrastructure and abused democracy.

Jayant was an aggressive, ambitious and a highly focused person with high levels of integrity and work ethics. This was a prestigious post and he knew he had to produce results. For him, more than the monetary aspect (he was from a wealthy family), it was his reputation and fame in his circle that was important. Jayant had built a small but a brilliant team of multifaceted professionals including IITians, Chartered Accountants and Management graduates from reputed business schools. Some of the team members were responsible for identifying and sourcing companies for investments while others were focused on Analytics, Research and Monitoring functions. A committee of four members was headed by Avinash, a brilliant, astute but an extremely greedy nerd. This committee was expected to evaluate every investment proposal and present them to Jayant for approval. Every proposal rejected by the committee had to be closed with a qualitative report. This would enable an audit trail at any point of time.

Being a Friday, everyone was in smart casuals. Jayant was looking extremely good in his white Chinese collared shirt and blue jeans with a fawn coloured linen jacket adding to his style quotient.

"Guys, we need to get into action ASAP. Between now and 2010, we need to invest a minimum of $100m and that's hardly 20 percent of the target we have for China for the same period. And as far as India is concerned, this is just a small beginning and we are going to see quantum jump in the fund size. We are now six months old here and it is high time we loosened our seat belts. The sectors favoured as mailed by me to all of you are Ecommerce, Education, Services / KPOs and Entertainment. Even if we make mistakes, let us learn from them. There are no restrictions on minimum ticket size, hence this could help us find more fish in the pond. Red Sand offers great growth opportunities only for those who are ready to prove their mettle with performance; others may kindly redraft your resume and look out for opportunities elsewhere. I am always available for help and directions whether am in India or travelling elsewhere. Catch you later, have a great weekend and await my detailed slides first thing on Monday morning."

After he left, there was excitement as well as tension among the team. Avinash realized that some strong message had come from the investing partners and he also sensed that that was the best time to encash on the opportunity available. After all, he had a dream of owning an independent villa, a BMW latest series, an expensive honeymoon trip soon after his wedding with his lady love in the next one or two years, a solid bank balance amongst other dreams. He craved for all of these within the next five to six years though successful investments happening out of Red Sand on companies that were to be built by the promoters through a lot of struggle, constraints sacrifice and pressure over a period of five to ten years.

Most of the discussions in the late evening party with his colleagues revolved around the message from Jayant. Fortunately most saw more and more opportunities that set the tone for a lively night with endless liquor and the scale of optimism dismissed the threat to the job, and Avinash felt that there was no need to redraft the resume and he ensured that he motivated the team to grab as much as possible from the market before others identified them.

Anand Ties the Knot

Time flew briskly. It seemed as if we had not yet recovered from Anand's engagement celebrations when in just a month, he would be married. The wedding was to be held at AVM Rajeshwari Kalyana Mandapam, one of the most prestigious halls in Chennai. Anand's father-in-law was very particular about the size of the wedding function.

On my advice, Anand had taken up jogging for the past six months and had lost over six kilos! As if to make up for it, Divya gained at least four kilos. Her mother cited happiness as the reason for her additional weight. Happiness derived from plenty of ghee, badam halwa, other sweets, fried items and day dreaming without moving a muscle!

The invitation card was almost as big as an A4 sheet, and much against Anand's wishes, his name in the card read:

Shri Anand Palaniappan, B.Com, ACA
Senior Director, FAB Consulting P Ltd

Thankfully, they didn't add 'ACA, first attempt'. Such a precedent would have put me in severe dilemma while printing my wedding card in quarter the size of an A4 sheet. Divya's name was written in the following manner:

SOWV Divyalakshmi (alias Ponni alias Lakshmi) BA Economics, MA.

The truth however was that Divya had joined MA through a correspondence course, but hadn't pursued it for even a month.

There were several names under the heading "With best compliments from", each having the qualification engraved as suffix. Most such qualifications had a line on top.

Since Anand felt embarrassed to give such a card to our clients and friends, he printed a very simple one that I had designed for him. At least a hundred cards his father-in-law had sent him were lying in the locker in his cupboard. He convinced his wife that he treasured those cards!

His wedding was scheduled for the first week of March.

The wedding was a grand event. It was evident that Anand's father-in-law used it as a channel to convert his black money to white money, as many rich and law un-abiding people usually do. There were many relatives from both the families, and some seemed to have planned to extend their stay and help the newly-weds settle down in their new life. Many thought that for a girl used to living in the lap of luxury in Madurai, it was a big sacrifice to live in a 1500 square feet apartment with no live-in servants.

The dark iron lady was in full form giving directions to all and sundry in the wedding hall. She ensured that she was present in almost 80% of the photographs taken that day. My parents were there for the wedding and were very well treated by both Anand's and Divya's parents. My father was delighted to get an expensive dhoti as a gift and my mother was given a Kanchipuram silk sari. I could hear her commenting to my dad that this was the most expensive sari she had ever received and that this was just the second silk sari she possessed after her wedding. My dad posed as though he didn't hear what she said on account of the noise in the hall. In fact, some of the family members were talking at a decibel level to outbeat the music from the two nadaswarams and one tavil. The small orchestra team believed that louder the volume of sound, greater would be their fee.

For the wedding reception, the clients and our office staff were invited. Special attention was given to all our clients, as times such as these help one strengthen the relationship. Anand looked the 'complete man' in a Raymond suit and Divya glittered in gold and diamonds. In this case, all that glittered was really gold. I was in a new blazer that Anand gifted me for his wedding.

In walked Neha, stealing the show. She was in a beautiful maroon silk sari with an amber border that had a little zari work, a rich amber pallu and a blouse to go with that. She had also worn matching but simple jewellery that further added to her beauty. Her hair was done up stylishly. I have always wondered how some women wore the right look on every occasion, be it at a wedding, at work, at the gym or at a party. Not just their clothes, but even the way they look changes according to the occasion. Most men look the same everywhere, every time.

My parents were thrilled to see her after a long time, and Neha made it a point to spend time with them, especially my mother. At the first opportune moment, my dad whispered to me, "Learn from her. Neha has the sense to work for an IT company immediately after becoming a qualified CA and has the sense to grow in the company."

It was with great effort I didn't let it slip out that I had had the sense to get Neha. He may have questioned Neha's sense in choosing a life partner like me!

At the reception dinner, I managed to find a place next to Neha and sat quite close to her. As my mom crossed us to take her place on the dining table a little distance away, she paused in front of us for a few seconds, making inane conversation – but I think she was already gauging how good we looked together. She affectionately pinched Neha's cheeks and told her that the guy who'd marry her would be really lucky. Was she giving her stamp of approval indirectly?

After the wedding, Anand and Divya flew to Singapore for a ten-day honeymoon trip, co-sponsored by the two fathers.

As promised, his father-in-law got him a new flat as a wedding gift. So long as Anand did not make Divya cry, he could live there comfortably. As if to prove how happy the couple were, Divya gained a few more kilos in the years after their wedding. On account of his migration to the new apartment in the posh Alwarpet locality, it was immediately resolved by FAB management (!) that Gautam would be entitled to an additional house rent allowance for a period of one year. Thereafter it was subject to renewal on terms and conditions to be agreed upon then.

ᘓ

Expansion Spree

There are a few ways of building a business and expanding it. One is to stay focused on one or two types of services as far as service industry is concerned and grow the number of users. This is generally very tough in a business to business environment unless one has a clear leadership position and unless there is constant demand for such services. For instance, basic 'security services' and 'house-keeping services' for corporates can be easily grown considering the number of prospective users if one offers efficient services at a reasonable price – but, for the same reason, competition can be high and can kill the business due to a price war. Since most companies in India look at pricing alone as a key deciding factor, the only way to remain in such a business is to create the scale.

At FAB, we also realized that mere accounting services would not be enough to grow at a good pace as outsourcing this function was a huge policy decision for any company. We were consciously adding a few allied services including accounts reconciliation work of various kinds, providing even temp staff for accounting functions and so on. This helped us extend our reach to a few MNCs who favoured such outsourcing.

During 2008, we extended our client base, which now included a mix of reasonably large Indian companies to whom we offered various accounting services on-site and off-site, SMEs and even a few partnership firms. For the latter, we even engaged in end to end accounting work. For MNCs, especially in the fast moving consumer goods space, we provided manpower to handle various accounting and back office operations, including order processing, vendor reconciliation, claims processing of channel partners and even employee claims processing. Though these were handled on-site at clients' premises, Anand ensured that he spent time to understand the various processes involved, especially since these clients used an ERP platform. This was an investment that would help us provide a completely off-site operation later in our business. We had deployed a team of fourteen to handle two MNC assignments. Our sales pitch carefully crafted all these services under the umbrella of 'accounting services'.

2008 was a significant year as our employee count crossed fifty and our company's turnover was inching towards a run rate of 10 lakhs per month.

We also realized that the best way to increase revenue was to increase the number of services we offered to our existing clients while adding new clients. There was a handicap though, and that was we did not have a presence outside Chennai. We realized we needed to have sales offices in Mumbai and Delhi and later in Bangalore. We had always dreamt of having operations in these cities. But we thought that this would remain a dream since the cost of setting up a sales office at these locations and engaging a smart sales/business development person out there would be beyond our means. A local resident would cost less and, more importantly, would have the required network to source business!

Our personal needs were increasing and so the need to expand and grow the business became more urgent. Anand was already married and was managing his life with a single income as his wife was not employed. If she were to work, her parents would think something was grossly wrong with Anand. In reality, he had nothing to fear. His father had invested wisely in properties over a period of time and he had additional income from other sources as well.

My case was totally different, though. I had only my income to fall back on. Though Neha's salary would, in all probabilities, always be higher than mine, I wondered if I should postpone the marriage by another two years. Little did I realize that running my own venture had made me more responsible! Would Neha take kindly to the delay?

Most of the times, personal needs drive us to explore and expand our revenue opportunities. Anand and I were no different. We enrolled ourselves with a few business institutions such as CII, MMA, etc., primarily to expand our contacts. We attended useful and relevant programmes, including lectures by eminent people. One such business presentation we planned to attend was by Vimal Chand, a business consultant who was on the board of a few companies as an independent director, especially start-ups. He was to deliver an address on the topic 'Growing Opportunities in India for the Service Sector'. Anand and I made it a point to occupy one of the first few rows (something I never cared for during my CA classes at the institute). The more serious or more interested you are, the more likely you are to occupy the front row.

Vimal Chand's profile, presented through a few colourful slides, was very impressive. Vimal was an MBA from one of the reputed business schools in India and also held an additional qualification on strategic management from an unknown university in the USA. Vimal had worked in a few companies in India in the initial years before migrating to the US. Even there, he had worked with a few companies from multiple industries – from financial services to health care to retail – before becoming a full-fledged business consultant.

Vimal stole the show with his oratory skills and presentation. He talked about various economies of the world, narrated the importance of the emerging BRIC economy and presented with conviction, the strengths of China and India. Perhaps his loyalty to India, being an Indian, made him favour India, especially as a BPO, KPO, healthcare and R&D centre. Anand and I were floored by his knowledge, oratory skills and the way he presented the data and analysis. We rushed to greet him at the end of the speech. Even if he did not give us his business card, we would have at least given him ours. It was indeed admiration and *awe* at first sight for us.

I remembered the advice my ex-boss had given me of getting a smart MBA in our board to add glamour and an additional dose of pragmatism to grow faster. And there, I could sense that Vimal would be the right person considering his background and profile, and, more importantly, his excellent connections in the greatest land of opportunities.

During the lunch break, while many were hunting for their salads, soups, chicken pieces and pappad like there would be no tomorrow, we managed to take a few minutes of his time. He was appreciative of our venture based on whatever little we could communicate to impress him, and he even went to the extent of certifying that we were in the right line of business at the right time and at the right place and that there could be plenty of opportunities within India and outside India. We couldn't have asked for more. It was a big relief, and our confidence level rose just like the Sensex does purely due to sentiments rather than fundamentals when the Finance Minister announces that India would soon open up a few sectors for Foreign Institutional sectors without giving any further details or without realizing the protests from various corners!

I took the initiative and checked if we could spend a few hours with Vimal when he had some spare time to discuss our business in detail.

"Luckily, I am here for another three days. Let me check my calendar," he said, pulling out his smart phone and checking the details. He muttered to himself, loud enough for us to be able to hear him, 'Breakfast with Sanjay, tomorrow lunch at Park Sheraton with Benjamin and so on....' Every meal, he was with someone, and that was a clear sign of how important he was.

"Great! Friday evening at the Taj Coromondal for dinner? Or better, for a drink and dinner?"

"That's really fine with us," I replied promptly as there was no need to check our calendar. Friday was just three days away. I was sure that Anand would have started making the budget in his virtual excel sheet for that evening.

"Guys, my sister may also join as she'll be there that day. Or rather, I don't know what her schedule is like but it would be nice if she joins us. I don't get to meet her often, so much of business travel... both of us hardly have any time,"Vimal said apologetically.

"It would be a pleasure...," it was Anand's turn to be proactive. "What does she do?"

"She is a consultant in Mumbai, focusing on the service industry. She is brilliant and has a good network in this country. She knows the who's who in the industry." Then, as if struck by a thought, he added brightly, "Who knows, if she has the time, she may be able to help you guys as well!" He made it sound like a privilege, and we were deeply grateful for his interest in our venture so early in our meeting.

"Done, we are meeting on Friday evening," Anand said emphatically, as if I would express some doubts. When we left the hotel, we couldn't contain our excitement. It was godsent and we could see a bright future for our company. We decided that we wouldn't mind throwing a few thousand rupees on that evening while we entertain Vimal and his sister. A few thousand rupees was nothing compared to having the honour of dining with such an accomplished person who was willing to help us grow faster in geometric progression.

ᔕ

Pressure to 'Settle'

That evening, my mother seemed more emotional than usual as we spoke over the phone. She tended to complain about my father quite a bit, and so the conversation was extended than usual. This time it seemed as if the dam had reached a breaking point so I decided to go to Pondicherry and spend a day or two with her. Even today I believe that people management skills begin at home, just like charity.

After completing all statutory purchases from Grand Sweets including a sari from RMKV for my mother that very evening, I took a bus to Pondicherry early the next morning. I was home by ten in the morning. I had to return to Chennai the next day since Anand and

I had to prepare for the most critical 'Friday the 13th meeting' with Vimal. Hence, I had just one day to plug the overflowing emotions and despair; I was becoming an expert due to experience.

Like any mother in the world, my mother was full of joy on seeing me and pampered me with an excellent lunch that day.

"So how is your business doing? Have you started earning well? You are already 26...and we are not like your friend Anand's family... we belong to the middle class," the statistician and the analyst in my dad reminded me of the facts of life yet again.

I realized that my parents would have discussed (I use this word loosely, for my mother would have barely got a word in edgeways) this topic at length and my dad would have blamed my mother's DNA for the way I had turned out!

"Not bad, dad, we are progressing well. We are now self-sufficient, and I am managing pretty well financially," I replied truthfully, glad that I had nothing to be ashamed of.

"For now it may be fine, but what about when you get married? How will you manage? I don't think you would be lucky enough to get a father-in-law like your friend." Now he was taking his analytics to a different level, comparing peers.

"Don't worry, dad," I replied cheerfully. "If what I earn is not enough, I am sure my wife will contribute significantly," I replied like the CEO of a company who has inside information that the probing analysts lacked.

My dad's eyes popped out in surprise and then returned to their original position. His reply in turn made my eyes pop out,

"Oh! You can dream on! As if a girl like Neha will marry you!"

What touching faith! And yet, he didn't realize he had predicted destiny with a precision that required no third umpire referral!

"Why not, dad? You have good taste! May your wish come true! We know the family anyway..." I said smugly.

But obviously, my dad thought I was teasing him and promptly proposed an alternative – an acquaintance in Chennai had recommended a girl. Her brother and sister-in-law were to meet me in a week or so. I nodded dutifully, deciding to have some fun in the meanwhile.

The next day I decided to leave very early to discuss the next day's agenda with Anand. We also had plans to buy expensive shirts and trousers and a new pair of shoes to make the right impression on Vimal. All this required some time, and we had only Thursday to complete all of that.

Before I left, my mom handed me a tempting mug of hot filter coffee and asked shyly, "Is it true?" This was perhaps the first time I saw her blushing.

"What?" I asked, buying time.

"A mother knows her son well," she said in Kollywood/Bollywood style with the same knowing look but minus the mandatory white sari. "Neha is a good match for you," she added with tears in her eyes. Some people can muster tears on all occasions, and my mom was one of them.

I hugged my mother, kissed her on her cheeks, gave her a few hundred rupees as pocket money (the generation of unaccounted black money starts at home for most) and rushed to the bus stand to take a bus to Chennai.

♌

The Amazing Friday the 13th

On Thursday evening, Anand and I pampered ourselves with new Louis Philippe shirts and Hush Puppy shoes. Anand still had a few new trousers bought at the time of his wedding, so I got myself a pair of new Raymond trousers. These expenses, whether or not allowable under Sec 33 of the Income Tax Act, were booked as business promotion expenses – cheap thrills, but thrilling still.

We went to a bar in T. Nagar after our purchases and discussed our meeting with Vimal at length, this hot subject was discussed over a mug of cold Kingfisher beer. We were of one mind about using this godsent opportunity. We were willing to do whatever it took to kindle Vimal's interest for some association with FAB for mutual benefit, of course. We assumed that we would gain more than Vimal because people like him were precious, though there were many Gautams and Anands chasing such Vimals.

On Friday, our discussions continued and we shortlisted the points-

- Entering the US market.
- Roping in MNC/large Indian companies as clients.
- Strategy to scale up business.
- Invite him to join the board of the company – though we were very greedy here.

We were concerned about the remuneration he would expect for the professional help he rendered, or even him accepting to become a part of the board. We were certainly not in a position to pay what we thought he would expect, given his background. But business sense prevailed and overruled our concerns; we decided to propose all these suggestions anyway and buried our concerns a few feet beneath the ground. At the end of the day, it was a business proposition and not a personal favour; we were becoming more and more professional!

We left office earlier than usual so that we could dress for the occasion. I was generous in using deo sprays and cologne and examined myself critically in the mirror to make sure I looked immaculate for the great evening. I had warned Anand not to apply any coconut hair oil that evening. At times, I become Anand's image consultant for free.

We even hired a Toyota Corolla to boost our business image. We did not want Vimal to catch us driving the Maruti Alto (second hand) that we had bought in the name of the company. At that time, we were too enamoured to even realize that we valued perception higher than facts. Instead, we enjoyed being chauffeur-driven in a relatively new, premium car – a heavenly luxury that would become a reality soon! I had to request Anand to remove the mark of sacred ash from his forehead (his wife had insisted since this was an important evening for him). Anand obliged immediately. I had also informed Neha about this meeting, and she wished me luck– "Have one or two bottles of good beer and have fun after the meeting," she said. She also advised me to be very attentive during the meeting.

As we entered Taj Coromandel, my heartbeat increased due to the excitement and tension. It was a great feeling to drive into such a hotel for a business meeting. A neatly dressed, tall and handsome security guard opened our car door! He wished us warmly, and as we entered the lobby, I kept aside 20 bucks separately in one of my pockets to tip him while leaving the hotel.

I felt I had arrived in life.

The hotel lobby was fabulous. There are several benefits of meeting people at such hotels:

- The place would be very cool, comfortable and quiet.
- It is a pleasure to wait for your guest/host because of the ambience.
- No one disturbs you while you wait.
- You get to see different kinds of people – Indians and foreigners.

- While most would be staying there on official visits at their company's cost, some lucky ones have the privilege of staying there while holidaying with the family. This builds one's aspiration levels.
- Most of them look good and very clean – both the staff and the guests at the hotel.
- More importantly, it gives a psychological pleasure that you are moving up in life when you wine and dine at such places for business' sake.

The only disadvantage is when you are the host and not the guest as you never know how much you will end up paying!

As we waited, I flipped through the *Time* magazine kept for waiting guests and Anand talked to his wife giving an update, though at that point of time nothing had taken place. In twenty minutes, we saw Vimal walking towards us. He waved and greeted us warmly. He was dressed in casuals – a lovely pair of jeans and a black T shirt. His shoes complemented the jeans. He looked handsome as usual, making me feel overdressed.

"Guys, good to have you here. Let's chat over a drink or two," he suggested. We walked into the nearly empty bar.

"So guys, what will you have?" the usual question put across in every bar each time and normally one of the members would be proactive. Vimal took the lead.

"Kingfisher beer for us," Anand quickly responded, knowing only that would fit our budget. Vimal ordered for two bottles of Kingfisher beer and a large Glenfiddich whiskey for himself. "My sister Ruchi will join us shortly," he said.

Vimal seemed impressed as we discussed our business. He quickly grasped the nature of our work, focus, strengths and weakness, unsurprisingly.

"Not bad, guys," he openly appreciated us. "A topline of over Rs 100 lakhs in this line of business in India within such a short span of time deserves a pat, and, of course, another single malt," he laughed as he ordered another round. We were high without drinking much. "I am sure that within the next two years, you will cross $3million," he predicted optimistically, prompting us to order our second round of beer.

"We need your support to achieve it and even progress much beyond it," I subtly put across our expectations.

"Oh! We will achieve it hands down! We should sell hard, tap the huge market that will be available going forward and create huge value for the company. It is a great story waiting to happen," he spoke in superlatives. "Ah, there she comes," he broke off and we turned towards the stunning young lady who walked into the bar. She was gorgeous and, as expected, his sister.

"This is Ruchi and...Ruchi, meet my friends and amazing entrepreneurs Anand and Gautam." We shook hands and she greeted us in a husky voice, "Hi guys, nice meeting you."

"So what would you like to have, fresh lime soda or a strawberry mocktail?" Anand became very solicitous suddenly.

"I will go for...." a pause as she thought, and then, "Absolut large with orange juice. Get me a pack of Benson & Hedges cigarette, lights," she completed her order. Anand was startled and couldn't come to terms with a beauty who smoked. Ruchi was tall. She had a great complexion that would make a peach jealous. Her flowing hair was cut stylishly with a few burgundy strands that carefully fell carelessly on the forehead. It was evident that she gave a lot of business to personal care providers. Without any doubt, she would make several Bollywood divas envy her figure and looks. She was in a bright red coloured T shirt with a liberal cut in the front and a black three-fourths. Even her footwear was colour coordinated.

I could see Anand's heartbeat going up; he was clearly excited to be next to her, enjoying a drink in her company. He seemed more interested in getting to know her, even more than Vimal or our agenda. He seemed keen to know where Ruchi had studied, her hobbies, favourite eateries, drinks and so on and was sipping his beer at a brisk pace. Anand borrowed a cigarette from Ruchi. He rarely smoked and it showed in the way he struggled. I was amused at his attempts to impress Ruchi by pretending to have similar tastes.

Ruchi lived in Mumbai, that she helped a few companies in building customers and sales and that she was excellent in networking with people – that's all I understood from what Vimal said. I couldn't get a clear picture of what exactly she did and blamed the beer for my inability to grasp the details. From what I observed, she was playing to her strengths and perhaps against others' weakness.

"Guys, this evening is just to break the ice and know each other. We shall meet again to discuss business as I can sense that you guys are keen to explore some opportunities," Vimal sounded us out.

"Perfect, Vimal, we can meet early next week at our office," I suggested quickly – we couldn't afford another such evening at a star hotel.

"That's a good idea. Wednesday next week works fine for us," Vimal proposed and Anand eagerly put in, "I hope Ruchi will also join us."

"In all probabilities, yes," Vimal replied with a smile.

"Vimal, tomorrow I need to go shopping. I am told a visit to Chennai is not complete without visiting Nalli, RMKV, and GRT jewellery in T. Nagar." Having caught our attention, she continued, "I need a vehicle and a driver tomorrow morning."

"Not to worry, I shall send you one. Honda City or Toyota Corolla will do?" Anand added magnanimity to his pro-activeness. Thankfully, he didn't offer to drive her to these places.

"Sweet of you Anand, that would be really great!" Ruchi was pleased with the proposition.

We left after a good amount of drinking, chatting, snacking and paying a hefty bill where the whiskey alone contributed to 50 percent of the total bill. Anand shook hands with Ruchi, holding it a little longer than required.

"Well, well, that was heavy flirting, Anand! I wish Divya had seen it!" I teased him. "And why the f... did you agree to send her a chauffeur-driven vehicle?" I asked, my irritation showing.

"Did I say that? I didn't realize it!" Anand said carelessly. "Anyway, it is all about ROI (Return on Investment), just like we spent so much at Taj," he added, as if I were responsible for it. "I am not a fool to focus only on Vimal," Anand added with a wink. We laughed and high fived each other – again, the number 5!

Red Sand Office, Mumbai

Avinash and his colleagues were to present to Jayant a report on prospective investee companies with specifics on the progress made so far.

Till then, only a small investment had been made in a BPO company, IndAsia BPO, a family owned business which had diluted 15 percent of the equity to Red Sand for better liquidity. The agreement was that Red Sands, subject to several terms and conditions obviously favourable to it, would have the right to increase its stake to 40 percent in the next three years. The turnover of IndAsia was close to Rs 40 crores at that time. For Red Sand, this was a safe first investment in the country. This deal was clinched by Milind, Avinash's smart colleague.

The team had managed to identify at least five companies, but nothing from the manufacturing industry. Two were from retail, one from education, one from foods business (a restaurant chain) and the final one from the IT industry, a software testing company. As they had not made any significant progress with any of them, they had to build a story through amazing slides incorporating various statistical data, industry reports and the India story to impress Jayant. They even had a mock session to ensure that all of them spoke in one language that would impress Jayant, or at least buy them time, an usual practice seen in such corporate meetings. Needless to say, the team was under tremendous stress.

A brief review of the operations and financials of IndAsia was presented to Jayant, but he was keener to go through the prospects on hand than dwell on IndAsia, as all was well with it.

Avinash took the lead in making the presentation. The initial slides spoke about emerging opportunities in India, changing economic policies and their effect on the investment world, favoured industries, the labyrinthine process in closing any investment deal in India, including the high expectations of the greedy promoters who expected huge multiples as regards valuation. The final few slides committed on closure of a minimum of two proposals within the next six to eight months subject to approvals and completion of all formalities.

After a brief interactive conversation, Jayant commented simply, "Not bad but not good." His opinion was as ambiguous as the situation warranted. He was tired because of too much travel in and out of the country in the past several days.

"Guys, closing two or three deals is fine, but we need many options. You have to line up more prospects as the final strike rate would be as less as 10 percent. Guys, pull up your socks and travel around. You need to start living out of the suitcase," he expressed his disappointment clearly.

"Jayant, there is a challenge. A good healthy company is averse to external equity coming in. Forget going for equity, they are averse to even discussing this subject. They need to be taught and educated gradually," Avinash explained, primarily to gain time till at least next quarterly meeting.

"Of course, Avinash, to get an entry and sleep in someone's bedroom is not easy! But that's our job," Jayant said cuttingly. "Be more aggressive and get hold of a few hungry brokers or syndicators who can connect you with some prospects. They will have vested interest as the commission will give them easy money. Once they are convinced of the benefits, they will push the proposal whether their clients really require equity or not."

"Got it," Avinash's mind had already started working – whom to contact, the network to be tapped and whether there could be any additional benefits for him. A deal is a deal, a win-win, mutually beneficial, in common parlance.

Jayant was still talking based on his experience, "Team, remember, to these brokers, it is like getting extra runs because of over throw in cricket – easy runs for the batsman, easy money for the brokers." Jayant smiled as he looked at everyone in the room. He looked cool or was pretending so that he didn't demoralize his team. He also understood the Indian market.

'And identify a few CA firms in the metros. They can be used as influencers! Their opinion matters to their clients," Jayant opened another path to tap. "I need to go now, I have a VC (video conference) call now with a group of investors. Let me spin a convincing yarn for them, they are extremely important for us; the funds they create ultimately give us the luxuries in life. Keep going and let me review the situation after a couple of months. And, mind you, if you complete one or two deals, even small, you will have others chasing you with proposals. Await that day. Slog like a donkey till then to live like a lion later. If you have to wine and dine with someone, do it, don't worry about the costs. Bye for now," Jayant swiftly walked out of the room.

After Jayant left, the team of four, including Avinash, remained silent, mulling over what their boss had told them. They just patted each other as they got up, communicated silently the need to succeed. And for that, they had to act fast and produce results. The time was ripe to exhibit capability and prove their mettle and in the process, progress well in the organization, earn fat salaries, incentives and great lifestyle, and create more vulgar wealth in the years to come, especially each time they succeeded in exiting from the invested companies most profitably.

A few other thoughts filled Avinash's mind. He saw more opportunities working with brokers. He foresaw more financial benefits flowing to him that would enable him to create wealth soon and have a great life with the beauty he was wildly in love with.

♌

Facelift of the Fab office

"Gautam, good morning! Shall we meet at around 8.30 in the office today?" That was Anand calling me as early as 6.30 in the morning. It was unusual. Ever since he had married Divya, who never woke up early, the till then early riser too had taken to sleeping till 7.30. Her parents perhaps believed that to wake up their darling daughter early would cause unnecessary stress to her.

"Sure," I replied spontaneously. Any second thought I may have had vanished when Anand also promised to bring with him hot idlis and Chettinad chutney.

"Gautam, it is important that we give our office a facelift. We need to create a good impression on Ruchi and Vimal," Anand seemed doubtful of our office standing the scrutiny of these stalwarts from the business world.

"At least change the order, man. Vimal and Ruchi," I punched his growing tummy teasingly.

"Yea, that's what I meant, both of them," he waved my correction aside. After a pause, he retorted with a punch line, "You don't get a second chance to make the first best impression." Ruchi seemed to have gotten Anand's creative juices flowing.

"But, let us not overdo anything, Anand," I cautioned.

"A few things," Anand seemed to agree. And then he went on to list them.

"Let us change the settee in the reception, hang a nice painting there, get a good side table and a magazine or newspaper rack. We'll change the commode in our rest room even if the landlord is not willing to pay for it (perhaps he feared a depletion of reputation in case Ruchi had to use the rest room during her impending visit). We will also buy a few good coffee mugs, get a mini refrigerator and..." He rattled off like the waiter rattling off the menu at an Udipi restaurant.

"Look, my friend, is this very important? It will eat away over 75,000 rupees from our account. If we start, we may end up even changing a few other things right from the doormat," I said sarcastically and panicked when he turned to examine it critically.

Finally, he had his way and as I predicted we, or rather he, went overboard. Anand changed the AC and even opted for a mini sized LCD TV in our room. He probably wanted to have NDTV Profit or CNN IBN tuned on when the special guests visited our office; all about perceived value. On top of it, the office got a fresh coat of paint.

Our Reserves & Surplus went down by over one lakh, thanks to Anand. Whether these expenses would be instrumental for our growth or not, they helped the likes of Hindware, Gautier, Samsung, Godrej and Asian Paints get additional business. A day prior to 'The Visit' – as I started thinking of it in capital letters – Anand gave additional business to the Landmark bookstore by buying a number of books on marketing and management authored by Philip Kotler, Peter Ducker, Ram Charan, Jim Collins and CK Prahalad and a few others, apart from a few books on accounting, Information Technology and self-help. But where could we keep them? So, a book rack got added to the list of his purchases, and the total expense touched almost 1.30 lakhs. This gave our office the required facelift, but our cash reserves was looking face down.

The office was ready for 'The Visit' and Anand was at the helm of the affair, oops, affairs!

Our Dreams Magnified

Neha called that morning. Since I had some time, I decided to speak to her. She seemed distant and morose. I was impatient to get on with the day.

"Looks like you are distracted," I said and that infuriated her.

"I am *upset*!" she said, with stress on the last word.

"Oh, something at work?" I thought, wondering if like my mother, she was also going to start cribbing.

"With you, Mr. Gautam," she said, startling me.

"What have I done?" I asked, trying to rack my brains for an answer.

"It is not what you have done," she said. But my relief was short-lived as she went on a rampage. "Except for a few messages now and then and even fewer calls, we haven't met in a long time and you don't seem to care!"

"Says who?" I said and regaled her with the conversation between my parents and me about my marriage and also introduced a white lie about how I am strongly holding them off. She laughed on hearing my plight and was surprised that my parents were more concerned than her.

I then told her about Vimal, and about how he could help us grow faster and our intention to strengthen our board. She was delighted and seemed to forgive me.

"All the best to you and don't forget your dear Neha when you appear on the cover story of *Business India* or *Business World* shortly," she teased me as usual. Though I knew she was teasing me, it whetted my appetite. And why not?

I must confess that despite my misgivings about the expenditure, the office was looking great. Even our staff dressed up well that day, as we had instructed them to. We put up some new posters as part of our internal communication:

'We love Mondays'

'FAB is full of FAB people'

'FAB, COUNT ON US'

'We are a team'

The office smelt good, thanks to the room freshener, though Ruchi's perfume was bound to overpower it.

I sent Vimal a message that morning to confirm his visit, and Anand did the same to Ruchi's number. Vimal confirmed immediately that he would be at our office at around 11. Anand and I smiled at each other, our hearts bursting with excitement. The BIG day had arrived when we would associate with reputed, highly networked professionals. We were on our way to becoming an institution.

Vimal called us as he neared our office and we waited for him at our little lobby. "Hi guys, good to see you again! Hope all is well," Vimal greeted us and we handed him the customary bouquet bought at the last moment.

"Yea, all fine," we chorused cheerfully.

"Is Ruchi following you or is she joining us later?"

Not in chorus this time. This came from Anand.

"Oh sorry, I forgot to tell you. She got stuck in Mumbai, some urgent requirement in Mumbai from her client. She asked me to convey her apologies and disappointment to you guys. She promised she will meet you soon," Vimal replied casually, unaware that he was breaking Anand's heart.

"That's fine, these things happen," I intervened before Anand could make any surplus statement on this subject.

Anand switched off the NDTV Profit channel while an analyst was explaining the shares that could be bought for short term, medium term and long term – after all, he was not investing. We spent the next few minutes presenting to Vimal in detail our broad focus, services, capability, clientele, revenue (top line) break-up, team composition, etc. It was a comprehensive download for him. Vimal again seemed impressed. In the meantime, coffee and biscuits were served by our office boy, whose dressing had also risen up to the occasion. After the coffee, Vimal excused himself and took a cigarette break in the sit-out attached to our room while attending to a few calls he had missed.

After the smoke, Vimal took charge. He picked up the marker pen and, with our permission (!), he went up to the white board to give us his point of view.

"Guys, I am impressed with the way you have grown this business. Pure play Accounting Services is a difficult business to build, grow and scale. Some big names are already trying to grab the F&A mandates from MNCs in India as these large BPOs in turn service the parent companies in other parts of the world, particularly the US. Hence it will be a challenge to get mandates from MNCs here. Even if you manage to get a few, long term sustenance may be difficult," Vimal cautioned us.

"But Vimal, our focus has been mid-sized and large Indian companies, though specific allied services for MNCs could help us grow our business. I am sure some of these services may not be attractive to these large BPOs due to their cost structure," I pointed out.

"True, but unless you extend your services outside India to those who can benefit from cost arbitrage on human resources, growth can't be faster and the business may not be profitable. Also, to grow within India, you need to have a base, a sales office, in Mumbai, and that's absolutely essential. Both of you are extremely strong and passionate and you have created a good team. I feel you are capable of creating and running a bigger team as well," Vimal remarked, massaging our egos.

"Thank you, Vimal. Coming from you, it is a huge compliment. We agree with you about having a sales office in Mumbai." I acknowledged before I added, "Yet, having a presence right now in Mumbai will pose some challenge in terms of financial feasibility."

"Gentlemen, being in Mumbai is not an option, it is a necessity if you have to grow," Vimal said emphatically. He then began to write on the white board. The first time it was being used since we put it up. He wrote in bold letters:

> 'SWOT analysis – Strength, Weakness, Opportunities and Threat.'

Under Strength he listed: young and passionate promoters, good team and decent growth. Under Weakness he listed: strategy, source of funds for investments and no presence in Mumbai/Delhi. Under Opportunities he listed: growth in outsourcing, cross border business and value creation and under Threat he wrote: sustenance and emergence of large names in this space. He also drew a graph with X and Y axes, plotted a few points and drew a curve that went up and down. He explained a typical business cycle. Honestly, we couldn't understand much, though the graph looked sexy. We were awed by the SWOT analysis, especially the listing under Weakness and Threat.

At 1 pm, we suggested continuing our discussions over lunch. Vimal agreed but he wanted to be relieved by 3 pm as he had already committed for another meeting. He preferred to lunch at a Chinese restaurant. Since his next meeting was at some place in Nungambakkam, we drove to Copper Chimney. All of us got into Anand's car and Vimal's hired car followed us.

During the drive, we discussed subjects other than business. Vimal talked about the growing subprime mortgage crisis, challenges in China and how value creation was going to work out for Indian corporates in the next few years. He was very knowledgeable and interesting.

During lunch, I asked, "Vimal, could you help us scale greater heights?"

"Sure Gautam, but I am wondering what my role could be. Obviously my charges are time based but I can't charge your company like that! I have to be fair. However, I do want to help you guys."

"You could join our board..." Anand suggested.

"Let us not hurry. I can perhaps become an advisor to your board and I can help you on strategy and value creation. I can also give you some leads," Vimal replied thoughtfully.

"That would be great. How do we structure your fee?" I asked, concerned that our inability to pay would let slip this golden opportunity.

"We will work this out. Give me some time and I shall get back with a surprise that could be a win-win for us," Vimal sounded as if he had an ace up his sleeve.

We were delighted and thanked him in one voice. Vimal left after lunch and we reached our office fully satisfied with the day's progress.

"Anand, though you went a little overboard in giving a facelift to our office expecting Ruchi, and though she didn't turn up to turn you on... still, good work from you..." I gave him a back handed compliment.

We laughed. We knew we should wait to see what Vimal had to suggest. We wanted to strengthen the board with a person like Vimal, capitalise on his network, evolve a better strategy and create an institution that would make all of us proud. I had the added agenda of getting a story about FAB in *Business India* or *Business World* and prove a point to Neha.

Anand switched on the TV again and changed the channel from NDTV Profit to Sun Music to watch Tamil film songs while I worked on a presentation for a client meeting the next day. When I left the office, I picked up the book *Good to Great* by Jim Collins, one of the new acquisitions, thanks to Anand, to read at home.

ꝺ

The Match Fixing

On a Saturday morning, one Gopal and his wife were visiting my office in the morning in connection with a wedding proposal. I had yielded to this unwanted meeting because of my dad's coercion. Though I had suggested a different venue, Gopal was keen to meet at my work place, claiming he did not want to inconvenience me! I was not a fool, I understood his intentions; he wanted to assess me and at the same time, gauge my office.

My mom promptly called me that morning to remind me of the visit. "Gautam, today Balu's son-in-law Gopal is coming to meet you. You remember Balu's daughter Vimala? She could be the right match for you. Hope you will deal with the situation carefully and appropriately. You dad wants to tell you..."

Either she handed over the phone to my dad or my dad snatched it from her hand. Suddenly he came on the line and said, "They are from a dignified family, well to do and cultured. Gopal is highly qualified, I think he is from IIT Mumbai, and works somewhere in the US. Talk with sense and ensure that you convince them of your suitability." I realized he was nervous!

I went to work that day with obvious disinterest. Saturdays were usually light working days and so Anand took off. Normally the first one hour or so on Saturdays was devoted for team interaction and some serious reviews on operations; that Saturday was different.

The meeting with the team leads in the first half-hour at least made me feel good as things were moving smoothly. If there were no complaints from clients, we assumed all was well and that works for most entities in service industry.

I sent a message to Neha to tease her, *"hi dear, pressure on you, someone is meeting me regarding a marriage proposal, am in demand."*

"Wow, all the best, this could mean a great escape for me," she replied naughtily.

"Who said that? you can't escape, dear…we are married for the next few births," I replied romantically and quite spontaneously.

"Love you and all the best for an entertaining session with the surveyors," that was from Neha.

"Ok, bye, I think he is reaching anytime now," I ended the chat for the moment.

Gopal and his wife entered my cabin. He introduced himself, "I am Gopal, son-in-law of Mr. Balakrishnan. I am an alumnus from IIT Mumbai and also a Cost Accountant, currently placed in LA."

"Great, you did your CWA after you graduated from IIT? I thought that any reasonably brilliant IITian gets placed easily on passing out without the need to go through the struggle of doing another professional course!" I was amused and took a dig at him.

It was wasted on this earnest man. "Yea, I wanted to get a good grip on costing that would help me, especially in a manufacturing or process industry," he replied with pride.

"And where was your first job?" I was curious.

"I joined a bank as the package was irresistible and I continue to flourish in this industry," he replied, completely unaware of the irony of the situation. Then he introduced his wife Jaya, adding, "We are happily married," as if he liked to score points. I looked at the sad-faced Jaya who was but a trophy. Her smile seemed rationed, and words even more. God seemed to have rationed her looks too.

Gopal's eyes scanned my office as he conversed. On his request, I took him on a tour of my small office. He made no comment but seemed pleased with the books in our cabin, courtesy Anand. When he told me that he had read and loved most of these books and our tastes were similar, it was my turn to respond with a rationed smile. Thankfully he did not get into a discussion about any of the books. Maybe he too only loved to have them on display.

"So Gautam, what are your plans?" the survey commenced.

"Nothing much, today being a Saturday. I go back to my apartment after having lunch somewhere on the way. If I feel like it, I watch a movie at night," I detailed the grand plans for the day!

"Nope! I was asking about your career, your dreams, goals, something like that," he said looking not one bit amused with my reply. I was.

"Ours is a start-up company and there is a long way to go," I compressed the usual macro statement in a nutshell.

"Oh, okay! How are the opportunities and do you think this will pay you in the long run?" he continued the interview!

"It is all about hope: hope is life and life is hope," I replied throwing a philosophical generality at him.

"Agreed. Still, one needs money, a sustained income, and wealth when one gets married, which is a life-long commitment," he stated the obvious.

"I agree. We are doing reasonably well and one can't build business without sacrifices and some compromises," I replied honestly.

"Do you earn at least Rs 10 lakhs a year? I am told that one needs at least that kind of a salary to have a middle class lifestyle in India," he was blunt. "Sorry for asking such a question, don't feel offended," he added, not at all sounding sorry.

"Not at all," I said generously. "I take home perhaps 60 to 65 percent of what you mentioned as there is always a need to leave cash in the system," I replied uncomfortably as my image was taking a beating. The presence of the silent observer with that rationed smile did not help matters.

Gopal was visibly displeased with my income, or the lack of it. I answered a few other questions including our company's revenue, relationship with Anand, my other interests, etc., that I thought were quite important for his review and assessment. Though I was least bothered about the result, I was helping him prepare a detailed report to his father-in-law.

"Do you smoke....and...drink?" he suddenly asked crudely. I flushed in anger but maintained my cool.

"Yea, I drink but I don't smoke," I replied with cold indifference. I did not like the way he was assessing me.

Gopal seemed equally uncomfortable with my reply.

"Anything you want to know about Vimala?" Gopal finally asked me.

"Just one or two," I said. "Does she drink or smoke? Does she party with her friends?" I knew I was rude, and I had nothing against Vimala. But I had to put Gopal in his place.

"This is very rude, Gautam! How can you ask such a question?" Gopal said annoyed. Jaya's rationed smile was withdrawn completely.

"I am sorry, if it was rude or hurting. Gopal, there are a few details that only the boy and the girl should discuss with each other. If it is really important for you, then find it out discreetly. Vimala can ask me, she has a right, not you! I wouldn't mind this question if both of us are in a bar. Got it?" My reply was razor sharp and must have cut his ego into several pieces.

He got up to leave and shook hands weakly. Jaya finally opened her mouth to utter two words, "Bye, thanks."

I was disturbed, angry and agitated. I called Neha and narrated the episode. She felt that I had been ruder than necessary. I told her clearly that I wouldn't take such crap anymore and that both of us had to broach the subject with our families soon, very soon. My mood and tone were such that my decision came out as a command rather than romantic eagerness.

Within minutes, my dad called me and poured out his unhappiness and distress at the way I had handled Gopal & co. "Who will marry you? You think you are one…." He searched for the right word, and unable to find one, he continued repeating what he said before he hung up. I listened to him as though I was attending a call from a call centre selling a credit card or a personal loan without knowing the background. I held the phone to my ear with least interest and attention till he finally disconnected it. I cursed myself for being rude and called back to apologize, knowing my behaviour would reflect on his reputation. It didn't placate him and he just hung up again.

That Saturday was completely screwed by an ass named Gopal.

♌

We got Mail

My old friends and I got together to welcome the new year –2009. Anand couldn't come as he had several guests at home – his wife's parents, brother, grandmother, aunt and her husband and at least four or five hyper active children. He had to be the dutiful son-in-law and hence he missed the party. It was an opportunity for me to catch up with a few friends after a long time. Many of them had moved up the corporate ladder. They shared a lot of information useful for my business.

When I went to work on 1 January, some issues cropped up. Some of the team members deployed on site were absent either because of hangover or reluctance to present themselves with blood-shot eyes from excessive drinking on 31st night which stretched to the early hours of 1 January. I had to answer all the calls – a euphemism for apologizing.

I was in a bad mood as I checked my mail in my newly acquired laptop. There were a few mails relating to sale of replica Rolex watches, amazing pills that boost your sexual urge and performance and a mail from Mrs. Martin from somewhere in Africa who had just lost her husband and had inherited cash worth $500 million and she had to move the cash out of her country for some political reasons. She had identified me to help her. If I helped her in this project, I was entitled to 10% of the sum involved. Poor Mrs. Martin had been sending this mail to me every now and then for the past few years. The mail from Mrs. Martin was written so emotionally that even Neha had been unable to match her intensity. Replica Rolex never fascinated me, performance pills were not needed then and hence irrelevant and I had no intention of partnering with Mrs. Martin though the offer was very attractive and lucrative!

Yet another mail grabbed my attention as the subject read 'It is a deal'. It was from Vimal and thankfully it hadn't got camouflaged amongst the mails pertaining to Rolex, sex pills and Mrs. Martin. I was excited and went through the mail.

Hi Anand and Gautam,

I am currently in the US and will be back in Mumbai next week. I have been thinking as to what could be the best way to associate ourselves considering all relevant parameters. It should be a WIN-WIN for both. The following could be the options:

- *I get allotted 15% of the equity in your company and I also join your board.*
- *No monthly financial compensation for me for the time I would spend in India or in the USA for FAB. Only a marginal 1.50% of the total revenue of the company could be paid to me as a token consideration.*
- *My specific apportioned expenses incurred for FAB on travel and entertainment both within and outside India to be reimbursed.*

I shall add value to our company with my participation as a board member especially on strategy, client acquisition, cross border business and help you guys in value creation. If this sounds fine, we can go ahead. Feel free to write to me in case you need any clarification. I also suggest that you keep this proposal under the hat till we finalize the details – <u>don't spread the news in the market now.</u>

Best,
Vimal

Vimal had underlined the last sentence to stress the importance of confidentiality.

I was on tenterhooks. While the proposal looked fine, the 1.5% commission on the total revenue was a cause for concern.

Of course, Vimal was extremely generous in not demanding any monthly compensation except meeting the expenses he incurred on behalf of FAB.

I missed Anand that day and couldn't talk to Neha too as she was in a workshop in the outskirts of Bangalore. Anand was chaperoning a team of 12, showing them the city. So I replied thanking Vimal for his offer and promised to reply soon.

A strong board, a brilliant strategy, scaling up business, dollar income and the prospect of building an institution – these dreams made my adrenaline flow. As I added small details to the dreams, my excitement built palpably and I visited the restroom more frequently (thankfully it was attached to our cabin). Unable to contain myself, I sent a detailed SMS to Neha, knowing she would share my excitement.

The offer mail from Vimal completely overwhelmed any iota of desire to partner with Mrs. Martin to create wealth for myself. "Sorry Mrs. Martin, your offer mail has again gone into junk," I thought as I did the needful.

I also realized that a day would come when my dad would feel pleased and relieved that his only son had turned out to be a successful entrepreneur. That day would be highly gratifying for me.

♌

Board becomes Broad

Anand was back to work on Wednesday. He was looking tired and tanned because of the city tour, which included several temple stops – right from Kapaleeswarar temple, Triplicane Parthasarathy temple, Nanganallur Hanuman temple, to Vadapalani Murugan temple; places of interest for the youngsters including Vandalur zoo, Guindy snake park and finally a few restaurants from Amaravati to Anjappar. I was told that he had travelled close to 600 kms in the last three or four days. Though he looked tired, he also seemed to have expanded around the waistline, thanks to the special food at home for the guests and the hotel food, and a few cups and cones of ice cream.

I gave him the big news even before he checked his mail. His joy was equal, if not more. We discussed the pros and cons and shared the discomfort about the 1.50% commission on topline. We thought we could negotiate and bring it down to 1% as otherwise it would affect cash flows. The 15% equity did not concern us as much as it didn't result in any cash outflow. But we also realized that by not asking us for a monthly fee, he was being magnanimous and we didn't want to act cheap.

We replied that day, expressing our happiness at having him on board. But we also firmly indicated that we could consider 1% commission on total revenue instead of 1.5%. Vimal immediately agreed, humbling us yet again. Anand took the initiative of reaching out to Ruchi to get us leverage in Mumbai. It was agreed that for the first one year or so, we wouldn't have any office space in Mumbai. Ruchi magnanimously agreed to lend her residential address as our Mumbai office address for the sake of having a presence. We knew that no client would be visiting our Mumbai office as it was just a one-man, or rather, one-woman business development office.

As compensation, Ruchi was to get Rs six lakhs per annum plus expenses. This suited us fine since she was not committing full time to FAB. Still, it meant Anand and I would take home less, but we graciously put the company's interest above our self-interest, as usual. Ruchi was also allotted 10% equity. This was on recommendation from Vimal, who felt that this way, we could keep our yearly pay out to a minimum while still moving forward.

It took us almost three months to complete the formalities, and from the new financial year 2009-10, we had a bigger, brighter, competent and a colourful board. During April, we held our formal board meeting, first of its kind for Anand and me. Vimal and Ruchi, our new board members, were present for the meeting.

A new structure and new targets were drawn. I was made the CEO of the company and Anand the COO. I vehemently opposed this and wanted Anand to be the CEO as he was more knowledgeable than me. But Anand firmly believed that I should be the CEO since he felt that I was CEO material. I finally yielded as these designations were mainly for external references. In reality, Anand and I were at the same level with no misplaced personal ego hindering the progress of the company or breaking our friendship. Anand never let me down.

The broad plan was drawn for the next five years, by when we were to achieve revenues of Rs 25 crores. Anand's and my eyes popped out as we couldn't believe we could achieve such revenues within five years, even if it was only on paper. Such aspirational numbers can drive anyone anytime and we were no exceptions. The estimated team size was anywhere between 450 and 500, with majority of operations being handled out of Chennai and partly out of our delivery centres in Mumbai, Bangalore and Hyderabad. We also discussed the means and processes of business development and brand building. I wished we could quickly skip the next four years and launch into the fifth year as life looked pretty great after five years, considering the projected revenues.

When the board meeting ended, we requested Vimal and Ruchi to submit their bills. They promised they would do it once they returned to Mumbai. Despite our insistence, especially a very warm one from Anand, Ruchi and Vimal could not extend their stay as they had to attend yet another meeting in Mumbai the next day. They left after lunch.

It was a fascinating experience for us. With two other people on the board, the quality of discussion and presentation had certainly moved up. We suddenly felt that from mere bean-counting we were moving towards something big. Vimal had insisted all along that an enterprise was built with passion, and that passion could defeat all challenges and hurdles. He was talking from his experience and it was very motivating. Anand and I were completely charged to take on our respective roles with vigour.

I decided immediately to break the news about Neha and me at our respective homes in order to settle down in life like anybody else; be civilized and create a new civilization!

A Prestigious Mandate

We had participated in an RFP (Request for proposal) floated by one of the MNCs for accounting and data processing assignments. Unlike a simple empanelment form or a mere letter or an email seeking opportunities to be associated with the companies for rendering services, RFPs are always a bit tricky and unduly long. Most of the MNCs have this practice and such RFPs are normally submitted to the procurement department in such companies.

This company was into foods and beverages selling packaged juice, water, some junk snacks and even biscuits. They were just five years old in India and as expected was growing at an exorbitant rate year after year by changing the consuming habits of our people through influential celebrities from the film and sports world who were their brand ambassadors.

We got a communication from the company that we were shortlisted and that there would be a discussion on the services that warranted a personal presence at their Mumbai office in Andheri.

It was indeed great news for us as we didn't expect ourselves to be shortlisted by such a company. We started to believe that this could be a game changer of sorts. Anand and I sensed that many good things were happening suddenly. The induction of Vimal and Ruchi was immediately followed by such an important mail. Anand conveniently called it 'lady luck', obviously on account of his attraction to Ruchi. We decided that we would put our best foot forward and present ourselves very well and create the right impression. For a moment, we ignored competition from our mind and believed that *only* we would be offered the assignment. Such a belief was to gain tremendous confidence in ourselves. The RFP was for services including outsourcing of the company's distributors' claims processing, employee claims processing, order processing, vendor payments and a few other tasks.

Though I strongly suggested that both Anand and I go to Mumbai together for this meeting to show our commitment and even strength, Anand suggested that it would be enough if I went for this meeting. He also suggested getting Ruchi to accompany me for this meeting. She was based out of Mumbai in any case.

We were supposed to meet Mr. Pankaj Goel, the head of commercial along with a few others as his mail was marked to some of them. I confirmed my presence with another colleague of mine without mentioning the name of the colleague as finally it could be Anand or Ruchi. We had just ten days left for this meeting.

Our name cards were redesigned and a simple website was also created. It was later confirmed that Ruchi would accompany me for this meeting. Our sales pitch was modified to appeal to an MNC and we had taken the inputs from Ruchi and Vimal too. Vimal didn't suggest any change except changing the background colour of the slides. Ruchi recommended a very few changes and asked us to add a few points that were not factual and hence we ignored her recommendation. We didn't want anything to be ignored for the meeting, right from a professionally created presentation deck to a mock session on Q&A (questions and answers) to a good dress code and even a discussion on the pricing mechanism. We were thrilled that immediately after the board was reconstituted, a new prospect was coming our way.

I landed in Mumbai and was received by Ruchi.

"Good to see you Gautam and man you look dashing today," a compliment from Ruchi boosted my confidence level. I was in a khaki coloured pair of trousers, a sky blue shirt and a dark blue blazer – all new! Ruchi was in a light pink sari and a matching pink blouse that had cap sleeves and she had applied just the right amount of make-up. She was extremely beautiful and even a dead man in the grave would attempt to get up to have a glimpse of her if she passed any graveyard on the way. I restrained myself and just thanked her for her compliment with a thanks and a smile.

We had to go to Andheri East and it was not far from the airport. The comfort of being driven in a Skoda with a sparking lady next to you relieved me of the stress and anxiety associated with the meeting. We reached the destination in half an hour. As we walked into the swanky office in the seventh floor in one of the tall buildings, many eyes fell on Ruchi and a very few on me. When we spoke to the receptionist, we were taken to the conference room where there were five persons including a foreigner.

The introductions got over. The foreigner was the global CFO on a visit to India. The others included the CEO, COO, National Head of Sales and Pankaj Goyal, the Head of Commercial. Everyone had a pleasant face except Pankaj Goyal who had a constipated look on his face. The CEO looked extremely striking and ideally seemed to be a page 3 guy. As no one was in any formal clothing, I removed my blazer and hung it on my chair. The initial discussions were at macro level that never needed real data, facts or validation and everyone participated except the 'constipated-looking' Pankaj. The CEO was looking at Ruchi more often even while I was conversing with him.

I presented to the team the brief history and credentials of FAB, our team, our values and our services. Special emphasis was also given to the fact that owners drove the business and our commitment to the business. There were a few queries and all of them seemed to be impressed and satisfied with my response. Once a while Ruchi also joined me in my explanation and thankfully, even while we had voiced a few subjects in chorus, we maintained standard replies.

"Yet, tell us why we should outsource part of our Accounting work to you when you don't have a delivery centre in Mumbai. Isn't that a handicap?" that was from the constipated-looking head of commercial. My reaction and reply was spontaneous,

"When the US could outsource tasks to India, am sure Mumbai can do it to Chennai."

"Brilliant!" commented the global CFO. I was thrilled.

"We also have Ruchi based out of Mumbai for any face time to discuss the subject you handle and any issue we may face," the page 3 CEO took his own decision and I anticipated more such meetings to happen.

It was time for the global CFO to conclude

"Gautam and Ruchi, thanks for coming and we respect your interest in associating with our company. We are quite impressed with your passion and commitment though your current size of business is small. We have reviewed yet another vendor and though they are much bigger, you have an edge over them simply because your company is run by Chartered Accountants and I have immense faith in CAs. So, give us a week's time and we will revert with our decision and plans. Remember, this could be just a beginning and the vendor would have huge opportunity as we believe in outsourcing and we intend adding other geographies to India too as we move forward."

We shook hands and left the place. With great difficulty, I hid my excitement and emotions till I reached the escalator and moved down the floor and immediately after coming out of the building, I just hugged Ruchi and honestly it was a hug that was for Anand. Thankfully Neha and more importantly Anand was not there, if he had seen me hugging the page 3 diva, he would have killed me and our photographs would have appeared on page 1 the next day in every daily.

We reached the airport.

"Oh shit!" I screamed.

"What's wrong?" Ruchi was visibly shaken.

"I forgot to take my blazer," I conveyed with real concern. After all, I had paid four thousand bucks for the same.

"Oh, that's okay. I thought something was grossly wrong," she normalized the grave situation as she had not anyway paid for the blazer.

Just before I entered the departure terminal, Ruchi received an sms that she showed to me.

"Hi Ruchi, nice knowing you. Am impressed. In all probability the business is yours." Anuj Chada. He was the CEO of the company.

"Thank you Anuj. Nice knowing you too and I eagerly await the association," replied Ruchi.

"Sure, more to come." – Anuj.

"thanks a ton" – Ruchi.

"hey are you a fan of Chloe, I could get that fragrance." – Anuj.

I understood from her that it was a perfume brand.

"OMG, you are too much. what a guess, you are really one…." Ruchi

I couldn't help admiring Anuj's nose for details! I asked her if he had guessed correctly.

"Bull shit. I didn't want to deflate his ego, he must be on cloud nine now," Ruchi winked.

"what's up this Friday evening?" – Anuj

The chat was continuing for a while and as it was getting late, I left the place bidding bye to Ruchi.

I called both Neha and Anand and narrated the entire episode, minus Ruchi's hug! Both of them hugged me virtually through the phone. It was warm, friendly and amazingly genuine.

After landing in Chennai, on my way to my apartment I asked the taxi driver to go through Nungambakkam High road where the office of Southern Regional Council of The Institute of Chartered Accountants of India is located. I entered the compound of my alma mater at around 8:30 pm with great pride and there were a few students inside the building. In the pretext of dropping something from my pocket and bending down to pick up the same, I kissed the floor like how Chandrapaul normally did whenever he hit a century. The comment from the global CFO was still fresh in my ears and I was glad I could offer my thanks to my alma mater the same evening.

Engagement in the First Attempt

Neha and I had charted the course of action. We decided that we would visit Pondicherry for two days or so combining the weekend in the end of April. Both of us reached Pondicherry independently on 23 April (five again!). I had decided to break the news at home around tea time and Neha was to discuss the topic after my SMS regarding the reaction at home.

23 April was a Thursday and we had four days in hand till Sunday to battle it out. But if the opposition to our marriage was beyond reconciliation, we decided to remain calm for the time being but ultimately do what we had to do even without our parents' blessings. In most Indian movies, the dejected and angry parents normally forgave their ward once their ward produced their own ward. To sum it up, if either parents objected strongly, we had two things to do – get married secretly and procreate to reunite with the families.

We didn't have the luxury of extending our agenda beyond the weekend for the simple reason that Neha had to report to work and even my workload was increasing as business was surging.

My parents and I were having tea in the evening at home around the very old dining table that must have been older than me, yet serving the purpose, when I opened the topic with some tension and apprehension.

"Dad, I think I am now prepared to get married," I initiated the subject.

"Very glad! But tell me which girl's parents would take the risk?" My dad was in his usual sarcastic self as he continued, "You don't earn enough to support a family. Your future is also not certain and as a father, even I don't know what and how you are doing!" Under that sarcasm I could detect concern.

"You always criticize him!" my mother came to my defence. "Our son has all the qualities that a girl would like. He will also do well in his career. His horoscope is strong," she called on the stars as witness. My dad didn't believe in me, my mom believed in my horoscope and I believed in myself.

"I will choose my own girl... and I am sure you will also like the girl," I quickly brought up the crux of the matter.

"Oh! So you chose your own career and now choose your girl. I am proud of you, my son! So you think you can find someone who will be eager to marry you?" he sneered.

"If there is someone like that, will you mind?" I asked him directly.

"Why should I mind? What right do I have to mind? You insulted Gopal's son-in-law! Vimala would have married you considering our family background! Now you are talking as though you will get a brilliant, beautiful, cultured and hard working person like Neha!" my dad fumed. But he had given me a golden opening.

"Bull's eye! It *is* Neha. We like each other (love was still not an acceptable term at home, not only before marriage, even after) and we want to get married." I sat back relieved after getting it off my chest. His approval was not too important though a positive response would save a lot of trouble and emotional outbursts, I thought.

There was absolute silence. My father's face completely changed from that of a villain to a character artiste in split seconds. I could see tears trickling down from my mother's eyes. I was surprised that her tear glands still had enough stock!

My father was happy because he knew her family, Neha was his friend's daughter and, more importantly, Neha was a brilliant girl and an earning member of the family under incorporation.

"Are you sure that she wants to get married to you?" my dad was still sceptical.

"Of course, dad!"

"But… are you in love with each other?" a strange question coming from him.

"Not really, we just thought we could get married as we like each other and like and respect each other's families," I explained with special emphasis on 'family'. He was relieved.

I sent an SMS to Neha stating that the green signal had been obtained.

Within an hour or so, we were surprised to see Neha walking into our home with her parents. Luckily, there was a smile on everyone's faces. Without speaking a word, our dads hugged each other and so did our moms. I wished Neha and I could too.

My mom kissed Neha on her forehead and cheeks. Both parents praised us that unlike the others in the current generation, we had given importance to family values and relationship for getting married. Neha and I realized that we had played the 'family trump card' well.

Like a climax in any Bollywood love story, parents from both sides were delighted, frenzied and very pleased with the lovers without going through the prerequisite angst and drama. 'Like each other and each other's family' had done wonders, where 'we are in love with each other' could have been a catastrophe.

The informal engagement got over fortunately in the first attempt without much hassles. My soul whispered to me that after my several failures in my CA exams, my bad days were over and everything would move on smoothly than I could ever dream of. Considering all relevant aspects, the wedding was to be held after four or five months.

ꝏ

Nitish signalled 'Amber'

It became a business practice for Anand and me to review our company's strategy, operations, pipeline, people and challenges once a month. We always made it a point to keep them simple, to the point and did not analyse much as we believed that too much of such analysis only resulted in paralysis. That was one such day for us. We were quite pleased with the progress for that quarter though we still needed additional cash for our growing personal needs. Still, we had no regrets as right from the beginning, the interests of the enterprise came before our personal interests. We believed that there was enough potential to tap in the market and we needed cash reserves, additional capital at some point of time for infrastructure and for investments in certain software tools, a strong second line and, above all, a non-depleting, non-depreciating energy, enthusiasm and the will to make it big.

Anand's mobile phone rang. I heard his side of the conversation. "Yes, this is Anand, who is this?

"Hi Nitish, great to hear from you, long time…oh sure… most welcome, come over, we are at …" Anand told the person the address of our office and briefly explained the route.

"Gautam, do you remember Nitish Jain? He was our senior. I know him from our CA days."

"Is he from the same firm?" I asked Anand trying to place him.

"No, he did his CA in a different firm and we used to see him at our institute when we attended classes. He is a very different kind of guy. I am not sure if he cleared his exams though he claims to be a CA. I am sure you will recognize him when you see him. He is on his way to our office."

Anand seemed happy reconnecting with him after a long time.

In less than one hour, Nitish was at our office.

"Hi Anand, hi Gautam, I am so glad to see you guys," Nitish greeted us with a broad plastic smile as he shook hands with us. I remembered him now. Our paths had not crossed much in those days.

"Nitish, we are meeting after three or four years, I guess," Anand said.

"After we passed out, we met once accidently at the institute and lost touch after that. I am really glad that you guys have set up something on your own and are building value through an entrepreneurial journey," Nitish had good things to say about our enterprise even without knowing what we did. He told us that he got the contact details from another common friend.

"Thanks Nitish, and what do you do?" Anand asked as I sat silently. Of course, I reciprocated the smile whenever Nitish smiled at me; it was amazing how he wore that plastic smile every time!

Nitish explained that after working for three or four years with an NBFC company, he and two seniors from that company moved out to set up and run a boutique consulting firm for transaction advisory services. His firm also helped HNIs (high net worth individuals) in managing their wealth. He was also an active trader in the stock market and must have made good money with least effort at such a young age.

Anand explained our line of business briefly without giving too much data.

"Fabulous, guys! I am sure I can help you when you need additional capital for your business," he was very forthcoming in his offer.

"Does your company invest?" I asked.

"No, we are consultants and we help in sourcing capital for others," he explained.

"So you are a broker?" I was still not sure as to what he meant by transaction advisory services.

"No, we are not just brokers, our role is much broader," he said without explaining what 'broader' means in a broad sense.

"Does it mean that you guarantee the lender or the investor with recourse in case something goes wrong?" I persisted. He did not deign it with a reply, maybe it was beneath his dignity to talk to a novice in capital market.

Of course, he regaled us with details of his company's general performance and dropped names. Of course, it was the first time I was hearing such names in the investment banking sector. No doubt, he was well connected and highly networked.

"And in case you want to identify any buyer for your business lock, stock and barrel, I can help you there too," he threw another offer at us.

I intervened, "No way, Nitish. We are building an institution and we are here for a very long term."

Nitish laughed and that annoyed me.

"Gautam, I need not explain. Capital is the lifeline of any business. The lack of it could kill any company however large or small. Moreover, for first generation entrepreneurs like you, unless you can exit within a period of time, you can't create wealth. Remember, you can't build wealth with salaries or dividends. And I am sure you don't even draw a salary at market rates as this is your own company," he put the finger on the pulse right away.

"Correct Nitish, but there are large business houses that have built enterprises for ages without an exit and we can also follow this philosophy," I argued, not completely convinced.

"True and I don't deny it. It depends upon the nature of the business, the industry, scalability, sustenance and the ability to face competition over a long period of time. Tomorrow, as we get bigger companies including MNCs into F&A (Finance & Accounting) space and resort to carpet bombing, you will feel the heat!" he signalled the early warning note.

He continued, "Don't fret, friends. My intention is not to scare you. You are my friends and I am your well-wisher and take my views in a positive manner. You are in the right line of business and I am sure someday a big fish may attempt to swallow you. You should get the right advice to deal with such fish."

"That sounds good and bad. Thanks Nitish, for your valuable inputs. We will certainly get back to you when we need such advice at an appropriate time," Anand concluded.

"Yet Nitish, we have built this company with great passion and we are emotionally attached with this company. I am sure you will understand and appreciate it," I explained with real emotions.

"Agreed, when one builds a company, there has to be passion and emotions but when one sells the same company, one has to be dispassionate and there should be no room for emotions," Nitish conveyed his opinion with zero emotions.

After Nitish left, we were silent for a while.

"What is your opinion of Nitish and his views?" Anand asked.

"Did you notice? He doesn't look into your eyes when he speaks! I normally don't trust such guys. Useful, but handle with care," I cautioned.

After a long time, the two of us went out to have a couple of drinks. But Anand had to leave as he got two calls from Divya within an interval of fifteen minutes.

Game Changer Received

Only an entrepreneur or a self-employed person can relish and cherish some of the highest moments of joy and excitement. Acquiring a client, even an enquiry from a prospective client, however small or insignificant, visibility in an appropriate forum or collection of some old dues that were on the verge of going bad make the hormones gush.

Business Ever As Usual (BEAU) is certainly never a beau for an enterprise. It is the ups and downs – like voltage fluctuation, though not at that frequency, and the sea waves whose trajectory is never the same – that add excitement to any enterprise.

At FAB, that Friday, 5 June was a memorable one, again the number 5!

We received a reasonably big, beautifully gift wrapped package by courier. The sender's name read SIPZ India! For a moment we thought it was some kind of a gift pack of the products of SIPZ sent to us for reasons unknown. Or probably because we had met the senior management team a few days ago, and one of them was kind enough to send this pack as courtesy. It was not a season for gifting!

Anand opened the cardboard box in haste. It was I who first identified the contents of the pack. It was my blazer that I had by mistake left at the SIPZ office.

"Wow, not bad at all! Thankfully the 4000 bucks was not a write-off!" I told Anand. As I picked up the blazer, a sealed envelope fell out. Anand opened the envelope and beamed as read it, or rather flipped the pages while I joyfully caressed the blazer.

"Yes, yes! We are there, well done man. Full marks to you," he exclaimed as he handed me the letter.

It was the non-disclosure agreement from SIPZ for outsourcing to us their finance & accounting services and all other services to be added in future. The covering note also mentioned that the contract would be signed within the next two weeks once the terms and conditions were mutually agreed upon.

Anand called Ruchi and conveyed the exciting news and he instructed me to call Vimal. I completed my conversation within five minutes, but it took Anand almost thirty minutes to do the same with Ruchi.

We called the entire team and addressed them that day, apprising them of the new development. This was important for several reasons. While the primary reason was to share the good news with the team, there were other reasons too as I explained to Anand. The team should recognize that they were with a company that was on a growth path and that their career path would shape up well. They could also infer that there could be some opportunities for a few of them to move on to the new critical and important mandate. More importantly, a satisfied and motivated team would always refer a few other candidates whenever the company required one.

The contract that we signed later was a game changer. Though it started off with a few dedicated seats for the client, the business grew gradually due to our excellent service delivery capability, efficiency and sincerity headed by Anand, who power packed the service delivery with a lot of value addition. In less than twelve months, we had built a team of twenty people exclusively catering to SIPZ, handling various tasks including accounting and various reconciliation tasks, accounts payable processing, multiple commercial transactions processing, MIS (management information system) and so on. The road map was also very clearly drawn leading to our handling their international business, especially the Asia Pacific region, soon.

After the acquisition of the SIPZ business, FAB gained some healthy flab as the team size grew. This resulted in a few more enquiries that quickly got converted to business. Things were looking bright and sunny at FAB.

Though I have received many more gifts wrapped in beautiful wrappers, that gift wrapped mandate was always the most treasured as it was a real game changer that enabled FAB to make trail blazing progress. The lost-and-found blazer was like the metaphor that represented the first step to FAB's growth, and it had the pride of place in my wardrobe.

ꝏ

Wedding Bells

Time flew without my realizing it. Gone were the days when all that I had in the world was time. The last six months were so dynamic and happening at the work front that I had no surplus time to pamper myself, party with friends or even romance Neha. Our romantic connection was only through SMS and the phone. Even on some Saturdays and Sundays, my extended sleeping hours and happy reading hours were replaced by preparation and review of reports, browsing for the sake of business and beautification of the Power point slides. Business was growing at an overwhelming rate.

Little did I realize that I was getting married in three weeks' time. Though we had planned to keep our wedding function simple, it still demanded some indulgence on my part. I was worried at my lack of enthusiasm about getting married though I badly wanted the company and companionship of Neha. I even checked with a few other guys in a different profession who had just got married if they too felt the same! Most of them stated that they were too enthusiastic till they got married! Perhaps the accountant in me was not allowing me to be romantic. I consciously tried to become a bit more romantic and the effort seemed to pay off. Left to me, however, I would have been happy to tie the knot in a temple and throw a grand party to all the invitees with the best of cocktails, mock tails and mouth-watering food. I had to yield to the standard operating practices (SOPs) set by the two families/entities and we had to map these two standards, reconcile the differences and variances and create a new process and procedure document that could be followed.

The wedding was to be held at Pondicherry followed by a reception there. It was apparent that over ninety percent of the people would be the same for the wedding and the reception and yet our parents wanted to host the reception. Independent of these two events, there was a plan to have a wedding reception in Chennai. The wedding reception in Chennai was primarily for our friends, staff, clients and a few other acquaintances. At my end, I came to know at least fifteen new relatives, thanks to the wedding invitations. Ruchi and Vimal confirmed their presence for the wedding reception in Chennai.

The 'D' day arrived and the wedding went off smoothly, without any anxious moments for any of us. Neha looked beautiful in both functions – wedding as well as the reception. The traditional *madisaru* style sari suited her very well, surprisingly. I looked like a clown in the traditional wedding attire, or the rather the lack of it, as I was half naked with only a dhoti to cover half my legs because of the *panchakachcham* style. The pundit gave me a green coloured belt with pockets to hold up my transparent dhoti and protect my modesty.

After going through various rituals, I finally tied the knot. At that happy moment, I noticed tears in the eyes of Neha's parents, especially her mother. For a moment I thought that she was sad that I was going to be her son-in-law, but I was relieved when I saw my mother also in tears – tit for tat! When I looked at Neha's eyes closely, I was surprised to see two drops of tears inside each of her eyes trying to come out and trickle down her soft cheeks that were pampered with rouge. She was looking even more beautiful! September 14 (notice the 5?), our wedding date was one of the most memorable days in our lives. Anand and Divya were there with their parents. When I introduced Divya to Neha, I noticed that Divya was wearing more jewellery than the bride!

At the reception the same evening, I felt more presentable in a wedding suit, and maybe even overdressed because of the mandatory jasmine garland with a few red roses. It didn't go well with the dress, but it had to be worn.

After two days at Pondicherry, we went off to Chennai for the reception. The wedding reception was held at Hotel Woodlands where several weddings or wedding receptions are normally held in different banquet halls on the same day. The food served would invariably be the same. On such days, one can see many Nallis/Pothys/RMKVs and GRTs/Nathellas/Prince Jewellery (the very popular sari and jewellery chains in Chennai) moving up and down chatting at reasonably high decibel levels.

Our dress earmarked for the reception in Chennai was exclusive to suit the crowd. I tried to look debonair in an expensive, custom-made dark blue suit and Neha, even without trying, looked her best in a peacock blue designer sari. She had spent two hours for hair styling and makeup at the Lakme salon. A sleek diamond chain and flashy high heels from Metro were all she needed to look gorgeous and admirable. She was, without doubt pulchritudinous. I was feeling damn lucky that she had chosen me as her partner!

Many of our friends were present, and most were very well dressed. I was equally glad to see many of my clients and my ex-boss, who had honoured me with his presence. Vimal and Ruchi were there, looking unsurprisingly impeccable and were the cynosure of all eyes.

Anand introduced Ruchi and Vimal to Divya and Neha. Anand kept a safe distance from Ruchi that evening, no doubt not wanting to raise Divya's suspicion. Yet, Divya observed Ruchi critically and seemed to be preparing a few questions for Anand later.

"Anand is such a helpful and a very sweet guy. Last time he helped me shop!" Ruchi opened up Pandora's Box without realizing the repercussions. An incomplete sentence is always more dangerous than silence! Anand later told me that Divya didn't talk to him for a couple of days. He saved his marriage by saying he had just recommended some stores and that it was I who had accompanied Ruchi! Divya immediately felt how lucky she was to have such a dignified and cultured husband and not like his easily tempted close friend and partner.

Nitish was also invited and he was there sans family. He was busy exchanging his name cards with many people who he thought could be useful to him in some way. Some people utilize every opportunity to build their network for the purpose of business even if the place happens to be a graveyard. Nitish clearly belonged to that category of people.

After a couple of days, Neha and I headed for our honeymoon to Ooty. Anand had arranged for an exclusive honeymoon package for us, one of his several wedding gifts to us.

Among all the gifts I received for my wedding, Neha was my best gift and I had many years to explore, love and enjoy the gift for the rest of my life.

♌

Same Home, New Life

We returned from our honeymoon and luckily Neha liked the apartment where I had been staying all along as a bachelor. Now I had to add certain comforts for a family of two. Out of some accumulated savings, I replaced my TV and the refrigerator. I also took a small unsecured loan and furnished the apartment. The windows wore curtains for the first time, the single cot gave way to a double cot and a small round glass top dining table was in place to enjoy the delicacies made by the new chef at home, with help from me of course. The second bedroom was also made ready for the guests, especially our parents. Both the parents, after 'helping us settle' in the initial days, assured us that they wouldn't disturb us for at least a period of six months. They believed that such distance from their wards immediately after the wedding was required for a healthy and happy relationship!

The joy was boundless. For the first time I discovered that Neha was an accomplished homemaker apart from being a career oriented person. She had managed to get a transfer to Chennai and had another week's time to join. Hence I also took the liberty of experiencing an extended leave of absence and continued our honeymoon in our 'new' home. Both of us experimented with cooking, and supplemented our efforts with home delivery and ready-to-eat packaged food.

We ventured out to a few places, including the beautiful Marina beach, Satyam Theatres, Spencer's Plaza and a couple of temples. Though I had frequented these places, going with your new found companion and wife was a thrilling experience and life seemed to be brimming with happiness. We politely postponed all invitations for dinners and lunches, including one from Anand.

The ten days of honeymoon at Ooty also strengthened our belief that we would be together for a long, happy and joyful relationship despite any hardships we may face.

It was the evening before the day we were returning to Chennai from Ooty. I was enjoying my vodka, and because of my good mood and the very cold temperature, I went ahead with my third drink.

"Neha, have one," I offered as poured one for myself, feeling guilty about drinking alone when she was next to me. Also if she joined me, I would have a good excuse to have my fourth peg. My mood was such and the ambience was such.

"No, I don't drink this stuff. Very rarely do I have some beer... And you know that." She didn't stop there, "Even you need to cut down on your drinking. I don't know how much and how often you drink, but henceforth there shall be rules."

"Oh my God, this is my wife Neha talking now! I respect your feelings but tonight allow me to have the fourth peg," I begged her lovingly.

"Carry on... on second thoughts, let me have just one drink with you," she happily joined me not for just that drink but in all my moments of happiness as well as turmoil.

"Neha, what kind of person do you expect your hubby to be?"

"Being himself first. He has to be a kind hearted person, have aspirations without being greedy, smart but not cunning and must possess a good sense of humour..."As I beamed, she added archly, "And it is extremely important that he loves his wife deeply."

"And what kind of person you expect your wife to be?" she returned the serve.

"A mystery that I want to try to solve throughout my life. Someone who gives me space and also takes space for herself and one who understands me and takes part in everything, good and bad," I replied seriously, maybe the fourth Vodka was playing the trick.

"And anything more?" she exclaimed.

"Yes," I said, putting an arm around her. "Nothing like it if her name is Neha..."

We laughed and hugged each other tightly.

The beauty of our relationship right from the time we were in love with each other and even after our wedding was that we did not expect anything from each other. We had no hidden agenda, no preconceived notions, no double standards, no judgment, and no artificiality. It was as though we had been living together for several births.

Ever since we got married, we ensured that most days we were back home before eight pm as the greatest joy was to nurture a sense of companionship and not compromise it for anything else, except on days when we couldn't avoid it. And as a policy, every Sunday we always did everything together, be it running errands, cooking, cleaning the house, meeting people, eating out, attending parties, watching movies or any TV channel. Even if it was a quiz programme in a TV channel, I also watched it alongside her as she was a quiz enthusiast though I hardly ever answered two out of twenty five questions correctly – she always scored at least 75%. On her part, she never refused to watch even a boring cricket match between Zimbabwe and Bangladesh. That is the secret of a successful relationship – participate in each other's joys and even sorrows (including quiz programmes and boring cricket matches) and we went on to create the path to live happy ever after!

♌

Misunderstanding Put to Rest

It was two months since we had married and we had yet not accepted Anand's dinner invitation, annoying him. So I told him to fix the date and the venue. The dinner was fixed at Kabab Factory, Radisson. It was a Saturday and Neha and I were at home as both of us were not attending office that day. We did a lot of cleaning that day and spent some time going through our wedding album though I hated my wedding snaps because of my attire and the forced makeup on my face, including kajal!

The second hand Alto still served the purpose of driving us from point A to point B without much hassle. We planned to change the car in the next one year or so. Clubbing our incomes easily enabled us to go for a better car by borrowing from banks or several NBFC companies who were chasing good customers.

Neha looked very pretty in a nice floral printed top and a flowing long skirt. The stilettos that she was wearing made her look taller by a few inches and suited her well. I was in my most preferred and comfortable attire, a pair of Levi's jeans and a black slack cotton shirt.

We reached the hotel and were warmly received by Anand and Divya. Neha hugged Anand warmly, much to Divya's consternation.

After we entered the hotel, we took the reserved table and opted for the buffet as a la carte would be complicated when you have two families trying to place the order just like where there are six economists, there are seven opinions! Anand and I had a clear understanding that we wouldn't discuss business during family meetings, and this was our first such occasion.

All of us were enjoying the dinner, we opted not to have any drinks that evening. Neha was very happy meeting Anand, whom she respected immensely for his capability, attitude, friendliness and nicety.

Divya was quiet as something seemed to be bothering her, maybe the hug!

"How is your married life? Gautam seems be the right match for you…" Divya finally opened up.

"Do you think so, Divya? Given a chance, I would have opted for Anand as my life partner. He is such a wonderful soul," Neha replied playfully. "Unfortunately, Anand is more like my brother."

Divya smiled but her eyes did not follow.

"Your hubby is extremely brilliant and you are lucky, Divya," Neha warmly complimented her.

"Yet, my husband is not the Managing Director or CEO of the company. Gautam is the head of the company," Divya replied caustically. We sat stunned, unable to react.

"What do you mean?" Neha asked tentatively.

Anand and I tried to distract them but the ladies wouldn't give up.

"Despite being the senior of the two and more intelligent – you know he finished his CA in the first attempt itself – he is not the CEO of the company," Divya attacked directly.

A heavy gloom settled on the table but she went on, oblivious or indifferent. What seemed to begin as a jovial chat was turning ugly. Anand was very uncomfortable, so was I.

"Not only that, it is my husband who invested more in this business but both are equal in this company," Divya was talking business now.

Neha got up. "Gautam let's go, I am not feeling well," she muttered. Her large, expressive beautiful eyes had tears which she tried to control. Neha's favourite ice cream remained untouched. I stood up and thanked Anand and Divya for the dinner before following Neha.

On the way back, we didn't speak a single word for a long time.

"Gautam , I think you must return the additional capital invested by Anand. Else, I fell belittled. Divya is right. Also, kindly change the designations. I don't want her to feel the way she is feeling right now. All said and done, Anand is your senior. Moreover, designations are crap and you know it." Neha was upset, and I remained quiet. Silence was always golden under such circumstances.

We reached home. She flung her handbag and flopped on a dining chair. She was in a terrible mood and felt very humiliated. She did not understand Divya's psyche or why Divya had spoken that way, that too to her, when she was not even involved in creating the company or the designations.

Before I could comfort her, the doorbell rang. Anand stood there looking mortified.

"I am so sorry for what happened. It was just a bad evening, a casual chat turning dirty. Forgive us." I had never seen Anand in such a state all the years I had been with him. I felt terrible too.

He went up to Neha and placed his hand on her shoulder. "Neha, forgive Divya, and forgive us. She doesn't know how close we are. She is new to this relationship. She is a wonderful person at heart," Anand pleaded and I was unable to bear his going on his knees. I left it to them to resolve the issue but yearned for it to end quickly.

"She is correct, Anand. I have already told Gautam to compensate for the higher investment you made and change the designations," Neha said without meeting his eye.

"Don't talk nonsense, Neha. You know me very well and please learn to let go," Anand said vehemently. "No one can come between the noble relationship Gautam and I share," he said dramatically but intending it every bit. "Even Divya regrets her outburst. She wants you to forgive her and is waiting downstairs for a signal."

"Where?" Neha got up and went to the door running. Divya was there, waiting with a packet in her hand.

"Sorry, Neha. I know you are all best friends and I shouldn't have spoken like that. I don't have such friends and I could not relate easily. I am sorry that I hurt your feelings. If Anand is your brother, then I am your brother's wife and I have the right to get angry once a while," she said, hugging Neha.

All of us laughed as our eyes melted.

"What is in the packet?" Neha asked Divya.

"Your favourite ice cream, fresh from Baskin Robbins. Let us not allow it to melt," Divya said coming in.

We happily shared the ice cream and when they left it was one am.

After they left, we both were quit though we were talking the language of love.

At the back of my mind, I realized that men and women looked at relationships differently. Divya was also right in her own way.

Business Soared; Relationships Soured

What was a lot easier even a year ago seemed to have become very tough then. The business was growing in geometric progression. Associated with this unprecedented growth, we had to manage other challenges including people management, hectic travel, several business meetings, and all of these collectively contributed to less time for our families.

We had more clients from the growing telecom, FMCG, automobile, pharmaceutical and even IT industries. From core accounting services, FAB also added a platform-based pay roll processing service. Many of our old clients moved their pay roll processing mandate to FAB. This proved to be a strategically great move.

FAB was already gaining visibility in the industry. People were watching us and many enquiries apart from those for business association, career opportunities, funding and even sale of business were hitting our inbox every now and then. Our very hectic business schedule and tasks gave very little time for me and Anand to leisurely discuss our business, let alone our families.

That day I eagerly walked into our office as after a long time we were in town and in the office at the same time. I had an agenda to discuss with Anand about taking some time off from work after the board meeting that was due in the next few days.

When I walked into his cabin, I could see that Anand was in a foul mood. He didn't even smile at me and I knew something was grossly wrong. I was worried.

"What's wrong? You seem very disturbed about something. Any issue at home, man?" I enquired with concern.

"I am getting disturbed with all kinds of fake claims from Vimal and Ruchi!" he said annoyed, still looking at his laptop screen as he spoke to me.

"Like what?"

"Travel and entertainment expenses. And now Ruchi is claiming a fee as a percentage out of the fee flowing from SIPZ. She is being paid a retainer fee and on top of it, she now wants a percentage of the fee from this client just because she accompanied you for the meeting and perhaps just because she has a face time with the client every three months," Anand's frown deepened.

"Relax, Anand. Both of them have always been claiming expenses and Vimal also claims a portion of this travel expenses to the USA. I think that was our understanding," I said, still trying to understand Anand's point of concern.

"But it doesn't mean that he can claim the expenses for birthday parties!"

"Come on, explain that one!" I didn't know what he meant.

"He has claimed a huge bill towards official entertainment expenses, and I know that these pertain to the birthday party he threw for his beautiful sister."

"How did you find that out?" I was amazed at his detective skills.

"I was going through Ruchi's wall on Facebook. I just wanted to see if she had posted any good picture of hers as she celebrated her birthday last week. There I saw a few pictures, posted after a grand cocktail and dinner party. From the comments that followed, I could make out this was at Hyatt, Mumbai."

'So you are her friend on FB? Wow!"

"Come on, Gautam, this is not the time for humour!" Anand was quite serious.

"Sorry, Anand, but why are you so agitated? We can resolve this," I said soothingly.

"It is not just these expenses. I have a strong feeling that some of his travel and other expenses are forged and we are being taken for a ride. I was also doing an assessment. It is over two years now and we haven't got any business from the US," Anand was using hammer and tongs on Vimal.

"Agreed. We will take it up with him. With them, in fact, when they are here. For that matter, other than some routine meetings with a couple of our clients in Mumbai, Ruchi has not contributed anything. There is also a cash outflow month after month because of the retainer fee we pay her," I added to the list of charges.

"She also has another company that is into human resources services where she helps clients in talent search and recruitment. She has been doing business with at least four of our clients and till date she hasn't informed us. I came to know because of my relationship with these companies. Don't you think that she should have, in all decency, disclosed it to us?"

"What! This is shocking!"

"And on the top of that, today I have received a claim for Rs 65,000 from Vimal and I see the Hyatt hotel bill too. This is ridiculous. It is not just about the amount, it is about business ethics," Anand was fuming.

"Got it Anand, we will put this across at our board meeting. We need not be on our knees. Let us deal with this issue professionally and don't take it personally and screw up your happiness. Just hang in for two days. We are meeting them anyway. Let us place these points at an appropriate time and please leave it to me. For heaven's sake, don't discuss the birthday expenses being claimed for the moment, let's not get too personal and too dirty by digging into details prematurely," I requested as well as cautioned Anand.

♌

The Board Meeting

As expected, the atmosphere at the Board meeting was not warm and friendly. Deliberately, we moved the venue of the meeting to an off-site location as we didn't want any nasty situation at the work place in the presence of our staff. Anand was a bit too obviously antagonistic, and did not even smile at Ruchi when we met.

Seeing the presentation for the past quarter, Vimal and Ruchi seemed very excited not only with the financial results but with our strong pipeline as well. They brought up the discussion on expansion plans.

"Let's keep at it, we are progressing well,"Vimal complimented us in his unique style.

"Vimal, we need to discuss a few delicate but critical points. Let me request upfront that you don't take it personally," I initiated the most difficult and embarrassing topic.

"What's that?" Vimal asked, unable to keep an edge from his voice.

"There are two things to discuss. One relates to the contribution from Ruchi and you, and the other is regarding the mounting expenses claims from you."

"This is ridiculous! We don't beat our drums with regard to our contribution to business!"Vimal reacted as expected.

"But Vimal, we need measurable contribution. It is now over two years since both of you got on board. Till date, we haven't got any business from the US though that was the implied expectation. Even Ruchi's contribution is very minimal. She hasn't got any big account so far on her own," I shot straight like an arrow.

There was an uneasy calm for a while.

"Guys, listen. I keep tapping international market with my network and that will take time and you need to be patient. Sadly, you are in a hurry. Instead of blaming me, you need to focus on building capacity and capability. And you must learn to appreciate the fact that I have been giving you directions as a member of this board on strategy. You should have the professional ability to understand and appreciate my contribution," Vimal turned the tables on us coldly.

"This is shocking and disgusting! I attend a few meetings on your behalf in Mumbai, and let me tell you, there are at least four major prospects that will fructify into mandates over the next few months unless something goes wrong. I am talking to them regularly," Ruchi justified her role.

"Vimal and Ruchi, let's put aside for a moment our professional ability to assess your contribution. You need to have the maturity to take our points of view professionally. It is a fact that we are terribly disappointed with your poor measurable contribution." I didn't want them to escape easily.

"To add to what Gautam has said, out of the total additional twenty odd crores of business since you joined the board, hardly thirty lakhs were through your reference. I repeat, mere reference. And look at the retainer fee to Ruchi and the ever mounting expenses claims from both of you. We need more accountability from both of you." It was Anand's turn to throw some statistics, and he didn't stop there. "Perhaps Ruchi is very busy building her talent search company and these are value added services to our own clients I suppose," Anand added fuel to the fire.

"Nonsense, we are shocked at your meaningless assessment, Anand. Many companies are waiting to get my name on the board! Considering the market standing, my education and my credentials, I have done you a favour by joining your board. Mind it!"Vimal tried to bluster though he was very nervous and even took some pill after that dramatic warning.

"That doesn't mean you book your personal expenses as business expenses. We are not used to it," Anand ignited the RDX bomb. For the next few minutes, there were heated arguments and several filthy words were exchanged.

"Stop!" I screamed. "Let's put an end to this episode. Henceforth we shall stop the retainer fee for Ruchi. She gets paid only when she gets new business, and for the time she spends on our existing business including meetings, she will be paid separately. We can structure this. Vimal also could be entitled to commission only on new business secured by him. A fixed percentage on the total revenue is not fair without any justifications. Also, we will draw acceptable rules for expenses claims. This cannot move on like this endlessly. We need to have corporate governance in place," I said firmly, ending the nasty discussion effectively.

"That's a fucking offer from your end. It is not done. We will get back to you with our offer later,"Vimal pounded the table. He was shocked that we rightfully questioned his contribution as well as business governance.

"And let me tell you, if things don't go well from now, we will exit from the company and you may choose to buy our stakes for a price that we quote. Don't worry, we will follow governance and ethics in our quote," he finished with flourish and the brother-sister duo walked out of the room. There were no handshakes or exchanges of smiles. Except the untouched coffee that had become cold, everything was hot in the board room. It was a bad day and we had to face it.

Anand was upset and angry. "Bastards, let them go! Cheats of the first order," he grumbled as he drove the car.

"Anand, stay cool! How do we buy their stakes if they offer? We don't have the means to buy. Let's not become emotional. Calm down before we reach office. We will handle this issue and God is with us. Now you drive carefully," I consoled Anand.

The Red Letter Day

After the board meeting, Anand and I were very disturbed. We argued for and against our direct confrontation with Vimal and Ruchi. Were we responsible for breaking up the relationship! Did we screw up the opportunity to tap the US market because of our impatience? Did we topple the apple cart! There were many questions. But these debates slowly gave us clarity over the next three or four days.

This was our business and we wanted to run the business in the way we deemed it fit. There was no room for hoodwinking and certainly no tolerance for white collar frauds. We felt horrible about our gullibility and allowing ourselves to be taken for a ride. No amount of additional business could justify the lack of internal governance. Unfortunately, we were made like that, our upbringing was likewise. It took us a knocking to learn this lesson.

In the interest of business, we decided to bury our ego. We sincerely believed that we could fix the seemingly broken relationship. We believed that we could still find a way of working together and progressing together with a new set of guidelines where each could contribute keeping the interest of our company in mind and that of our bloated egos lower on the rung.

After a discussion between us, I wrote a mail to Vimal.

Hi Vimal

At the outset, we are sorry if we hurt your feelings; that was never our intention. Our objective was not to throw any allegations against you and Ruchi. It was just one or two business issues that we wanted to put across to you and it was unfortunate that it took a completely different turn. I am sure we can put this aside and move forward from here.

To ensure that our relationship is clearly a win-win, let us draw some guidelines and a code of conduct.

We suggest that we stop the monthly retainer fee to Ruchi for the moment. It is quite some time since we took an office space for our operations and we have not been using Ruchi's space. She hardly spends any material time for the company for us to pay her such a fat retainer fee; we can easily hire a good business development manager in Mumbai who could devote the entire time for FAB.

We need to curb the mounting travel and entertainment expenses that you claim periodically.You are the best judge to review and get back on something that could be mutually accepted.

Needless to mention, for every new business either of you clinches on behalf of FAB, we shall agree on acceptable referral fee on a case to case basis. End of the day, both of you are shareholders and I am sure you would look at the big picture.We request your complete understanding, faith and cooperation.

Let us bury our bitter differences and move forward with better thoughts. Kindly convey our message to Ruchi as well.

Look forward to your reply.

Gautam

Anand read through this as I typed this mail. After it was sent, he asked me, "Did I over react to the situation? Should I have ignored it? Did I mess up, be candid in your views…"

I realized that Anand was feeling miserable.

"Absolutely not Anand, we think a hundred times before we enjoy some additional perks, leave alone drawing an additional sum for ourselves. It is just that we have been doing extremely well in the last two years and nothing is certain in business. We need to conserve cash for the rainy days and we have always placed company's interest above our interests. We cannot tolerate some jokers to exploit us consistently. Maybe, we got into the commercial arrangement a lot quicker than needed. We never consulted anyone else and never did any background check or referral check on them, but that's the way we are. All of it was done in good faith at that point of time," I comforted Anand.

"Look Anand, it is better late than never. At least from now, we will negotiate better commercial terms with them. 25% of the equity is gone; we allotted them such a good stake for just their names and just for the faith we had in them. And Anand, we also need to take the blame on ourselves and remember, we invited them into our company. You will agree that our inability to pay them well made us immediately agree for such a huge allotment of shares to them. We were worried about cash outflows as allotment of equity didn't remove cash from our chest. There is a popular saying – penny wise pound foolish. We are no different"

"I totally agree, there are no two ways about it. What do you think will be Vimal's reaction?" Anand still looked anxious.

"There could be a few options. I strongly believe that they will agree to our terms with some changes though. Second, they may not agree at all and we may have to carry on in this fashion for a while, say another year at least. Third, they may like to exit provided we give them an exit," I explained trying to think this through.

"But how do we let them exit?" exclaimed Anand.

"My dear friend, we didn't do any major homework or analysis when we entered. Don't worry, we will be led to the exit by divine guidance."

"You are suddenly turning philosophical!"

"There is no other option."

Anand laughed when I said this. I too joined him without revealing my worries and concerns to him.

ℓ

Avinash Under Pressure

Avinash's aggression was still not producing the desired results. During the last several months he had networked with a few consultants and even brokers who easily could portray as professional consultants. He knew that the best way to find a few investee companies could be through these consultants.

Avinash had successfully identified six companies that could be potential investee companies, and yet he was fully aware that in investment banking business, nothing was sure till the money actually got transferred to the investee company. He had to crack at least two or more deals to prove his mettle. His performance was closely watched and he was under the scanner.

He had an important meeting that day. The MD and CEO of IndAsia Solutions, a mid-sized BPO, was meeting him to discuss some funding requirement. After Milind left Red Sand, Avinash had become the contact point for IndAsia.

Avinash chose to meet the CEO of the company at their office in Malad as that was his first visit to the IndAsia office. One of the objectives of going there was also to get a pulse of the infrastructure, people, level of activity and environment. And this was the first time he would be meeting Deepak personally.

For the meeting scheduled at 10.30, Avinash was there at 10.15 itself. He had a brief chat with a not-so-good-looking receptionist when the CEO walked into the reception to receive Anand.

"Hi, I am Deepak. Nice to meet you, Avinash, and thanks for coming."

"Pleasure is mine, Deepak. I must thank you for calling me."

Deepak Manjrekar was the MD and CEO and the significant shareholder of IndAsia Solutions, which was essentially a Business Process Management Services Company that was into several services including HR outsourcing including, payroll processing and finance and accounting services. They had set up a call centre mainly for domestic business though they had recently succeeded in getting business from outside the country as well.

Deepak was in his early forties and was very suave. Anybody would get impressed by the way he carried himself. His attire, his body language and gruff voice was highly impressive. For a company that was set up fifteen years ago, they had achieved a turnover of over eighty-five crores. The growth had been rapid during the last three years, though. Red Sand had bought equity of 15% in IndAsia and luckily the company's performance became better after the investment, though Red Sand had played no significant role in it. Deepak though was sentimentally attached to Red Sand as he saw significant growth post dilution.

Deepak made a brief presentation on the company's progress, financials, people and goals. It was essentially a family business where Deepak and his brothers held maximum equity, although they had been managing it professionally and were hands on. The only external shareholder was Red Sand. Deepak's younger brother headed the operations.

"So you want to touch the magic figure of two hundred and fifty crores soon and thereafter look to unlock value through an IPO or part sale?"

Avinash couldn't help admiring Deepak's hunger.

"We know, Avinash, that to grow organically and become double of what we are today would be a time bound process. We are open for inorganic means to reach that number. Once we get there, the value of our company would be significantly higher. We are open for acquisitions," Deepak was very clear about what he wanted. "We need your services in identifying some companies for acquisition and we would also need funds for such buy-outs. Your entity could step in and we can progress together in our IPO dream and create wealth."

"Sounds good, Deepak. I am sure we will sign a deal very soon," Avinash spoke with confidence. Deepak's entity had the potential to get more funding, which would mean more business sourced by Avinash. If later they succeeded in unlocking value through IPO or otherwise, Avinash could also gain significantly through incentives. Avinash's excitement magnified. "And Deepak, since you are in multiple services, you must be open to acquire companies that are relatively smaller yet growing in their respective space. Ideally, you must look at companies where, after acquisition, you are able to make one plus one three if not four. Your multiple would go up as your top line grows and breaches a landmark number."

'Good point, Avinash, I agree."Then he asked, "Would you like to see our facilities and meet a few from the leadership team?"

"Not now Deepak, let people not get any wrong message. They shouldn't get the feeling that something is cooking. We have ample time for it."

"Good point. You are sharp. I like you," Deepak appreciated Avinash.

They shook hands firmly.

"So, Deepak, let us complete a few formalities and soon we will start the process. You may have to visit our office too and I shall introduce you to our country head sometime."

"Pleasure, Avinash, thanks once again for coming and... Avinash, let's catch up during a weekend. We should chat over a drink."

"That's an offer I can't reject. Next weekend, I shall contact you. Bye Deepak."

Avinash left with a smile.

"I should do something here and I will do it," he told himself as he drove from Malad to BKC, Bandra.

A Decision to Exit but not Retire

The dawn of that Saturday was exhilarating. There were a few reasons for it, or, we were capable enough to create reasons for it. As Neha was not working that day, she decided to get some chores out of the way – one of them being her usual bimonthly visit to a beauty salon to add beauty to her beauty! I had to go to work for a few hours. Post lunch, we planned to drive down the ECR (East Coast Road) to Pondicherry and stay at Mahindra Zest, a lovely beach resort. After some fun at the resort, we planned to visit our parents on Sunday and return to Chennai on Monday early morning.

This programme was to celebrate in a small way our new acquisition, a Toyota Innova, that was bought by me just a couple of months back and the new apartment we had booked in the most happening OMR (Old Mahabalipuram Road, the IT corridor of Chennai) and also share the good news in person with our parents. Though a lending bank in reality owned over 75% of the apartment because of our heavy borrowing, still we were the owners of the upcoming apartment, another addition to the population thriving out of the EMI economy.

On my way to my office, I had to drop in at my ex boss's residence as he had been asking me to meet him and I wanted to honour his request. I chose that Saturday as it was an easy day for both of us. He was extremely pleased to meet me and introduced me to his folks as one of his most successful and enterprising students! He also briefed me on the changes that had taken place in his partnership structure; a new young chartered accountant had been brought in as a partner. The competition from many emerging firms had compelled them to hire young talent, I thought. He enquired about my business and I shared limited information considering what we were going through. He was very proud of us and as I was leaving, told me that one of his recently acquired clients was in high end accounting business and that they had recently tied up with a Mumbai based company for some seed capital as well as business generation. It was perhaps a strategic investment. He told me that he would share the name of the Mumbai based company later as he was unable to recollect the name just then, except that the name was that of a very popular Indian cricketer. I just nodded politely, wondering why he thought it would interest me!

In office, the atmosphere was jovial and colourful. Every team had delivered great stuff that week and there were a few appreciation mails from some clients. Diwali was just a couple of days away and every team member was dressed in ethnic wear. Even most of the resources deployed on site were present that day at office.

It was going on so well till the mail from Vimal tainted the sheen. It was not copied to Anand, though it was copied to Ruchi.

Gautam,

Got your mail. Both of us are completely disappointed with your approach and logic. We got into your company purely because of your invitation. You guys seem to lack the basic business sense as you are unable to assess our contribution and you are also in a hurry. We don't agree with your recommendation, be it on the retainer fee to Ruchi or on the expenses reimbursements. You seem to be totally unaware of what the market could pay us.

Having reached the stumbling block, we can only look at the option of exiting from your company in case you are capable of buying the shares we hold. Else, we shall just continue as shareholders and our Board representation would continue to safeguard our interests.

Ruchi will continue to draw her retainer fee till June 2012 as her contract is valid till then.

Last but not the least, in case you need any help in identifying a buyer for your company, let me know and I could render professional services – for a fee of course; there is no room for free lunch.

VIMAL
RUCHI

I read the mail twice and later read it out to Anand. Suddenly there was gloom. The colour in the atmosphere faded, we seemed to have lost our independence!!!

"What do we do?" Anand was really concerned and he was needlessly feeling guilty that he was the reason for this chaotic situation.

"Look at the irony. The people who are on the wrong side are aggressive and carry such an attitude and arrogance and look at you, Anand! You have been on the right side and you have raised points on governance and you feel insignificant. And the biggest joke is that you are made to feel guilty!"

"That's fine, let business sense prevail. Shall I meet them and apologize and pacify them? Perhaps we can agree to their terms and keep moving as long as our business allows us to do so?" Anand suggested.

I was still reading the mail and something rang a bell. I kept looking at the names 'VIMAL' and 'RUCHI' mentioned in capital letters in the mail. The first two letters from each of their names when clubbed sounded very interesting. I wrote in on a piece of paper. It was VIRU. "Oh my God, this is the name of the dashing cricketer Sehwag! Could this be the name that my ex-boss was unable to recall? Can't be ruled out," I thought. I went out of the cabin and spoke to my ex-boss and reconfirmed if the name he was unable to recollect was 'VIRU'. "Brilliant, Gautam," he appreciated warmly, no doubt thinking how insightful I was. He added that the promoters of VIRU Consulting were Vimal and Ruchi!

I explained the latest discovery to Anand. He was also shocked.

"Screw them. Let us get rid of the leeches! The blood suckers! Business sense should not result in nonsense. From fake claims to relationships with our clients for other business, they have even associated themselves with someone who could be our competitor!"

"What do you mean, do we buy their stakes?" Anand was obviously excited with the spurt in my emotions.

"We may not be able to afford it. Our turnover is close to thirty crores and am sure they will expect a price that we can't afford to pay. Even if you assume a valuation of Rs 30 crores, we need to pay over seven crores to buy their stakes. Even if we kill ourselves, we can't invest that kind of money in buying back the equity!" I said.

"So, why can't we just continue in this fashion? In any case, we have to keep paying Ruchi till June next," Anand sounded defeated.

"No, we can't build a company where you are uncomfortable with the 25% share holders. Their contribution would dip further to oblivion in just a matter of time. And I am sure we will feel depressed if and when we reach the landmark figure of one hundred crores topline. Remember you will still own only 75% at that point of time. Let's face the problem right away."

"Meaning?!" Anand sought an explanation.

"Let's sell our company and exit," I spoke as though someone was waiting to buy us out.

"Will they agree to sell their stakes?" Anand asked doubtfully.

"Why not? They have lost interest in us. They would love to move away with whatever they get. If you win a lottery, every rupee you get is cash won for literally nothing," I elucidated it simply.

"Why can't we find someone who can buy only their stakes?" Anand gave a good suggestion.

"Not a bad idea. Yet, imagine, these two walk away with a few crores and we continue to slog like donkeys and live each day with the hope that we would also make some wealth that we deserve at some point of time! Will this work? What if we don't get an exit option for another ten years? There is no certainty in any business, right? If we fail to exit later, let me tell you Anand, we would become the laughing stock for having enabled someone make quick wealth at our cost. And there is no assurance that the new 25% stake holder would add comfort to your way of working." Somehow I was unable to come to terms with Anand's suggestion.

"That's not the issue, Gautam. Let's get rid of them and we have several years to work. We are very young to exit and retire. In any case, these two have to be paid their dues at some point of time. Let's not fret about what they make, let's worry about ourselves"

"Okay, buddy, let me go along with your idea. Let's identify some buyers and see the pulse. And mind you, even if we exit completely, we are not retiring..."

Suddenly the challenges and disappointments made us stronger.

"Call Nitish later for a meeting and let's take his advice as well as his services. Let him meet us on Monday in the second half," I requested Anand.

"You carry on with your Pondicherry trip. Don't cancel the programme because of this mess we are going through," Anand was concerned again.

"No way, my dear friend. Our personal happiness and pleasure cannot be fucked by such external factors. Life has to move on and it looks like we are in for better days… Don't forget to call Nitish."

I left the office, looking forward to a good drive on a nice road with a lovely companion to a beautiful place…

♌

Finding a Buyer

Nitish was expected that day post lunch. Anand and I had had a few days in between to discuss our strategy with caution. We were no longer single, we were married and settled as per popular definition! There was no point in unsettling ourselves due to emotional reasons at work. We knew it wouldn't help anyone's cause. Moreover, Anand was going to become a father soon, and every month I also dreaded the prospect of becoming a father!

I narrated the entire episode to Neha during our drive from Chennai to Pondicherry and she agreed with the decision Anand and I took. Her only advice was that I should not later regret whatever decision I took. "Do as your heart says," she said. "There are fallacies associated with most start-ups and the price has to be paid. You have done well and there should be no room for any regret. Mind you, this is very common in business and don't mix business equations with personal emotions." Neha's words comforted me. When Anand appraised Divya, she was excited and hoped that once this entity was sold, Anand could then get into real business; Accounting Services seemed outside that purview.

We had three options as discussed between us several times. One was to beg, borrow or steal and buy their stakes, the second was to continue status quo by sorting out the issues and the third was to look out for a total exit. We opted to exit since even a reasonable valuation would require a few crores to be paid to Vimal and Ruchi to buy their collective twenty-five percent holding in the company. Maintaining status quo was out of choice as we had completely lost faith in them and their attitude would kill us each day. Exit seemed the only way out.

At three sharp, Nitish came to meet us as scheduled.

"Nitish, thanks for coming. We are toying with some ideas… to dilute our stake now, look out for a buyer for Vimal and Ruchi's stakes alone and continue to run the company or go for a 100 percent exit. What do you advice?" Anand asked Nitish.

We didn't explain the entire episode to Nitish, after all there was no necessity to share our internal issues threadbare.

"It is a good time for exiting, Anand. I don't think you should look for part dilution as there are already four shareholders in your company. Moreover, anyone wanting a stake in your company would prefer to be a majority stakeholder," Nitish was quick to respond.

"So what should we do? What kind of buyer do you recommend?" Anand continued the discussion as I maintained the minutes.

"Ideally a strategic buyer rather than a financial investor. The valuation could be better if it is a strategic buyer as a strategic buyer would offer a better multiple than a mere financial investor," Nitish said from experience.

"Great. A strategic buyer may not prefer us to continue with them after acquisition, I suppose?" I threw a point at Nitish.

"Can't say. Yet, I doubt if you would want to continue after you cease to be the owners," he returned with a valid point of view.

We knew he was talking much sense.

"Do you think we could initially push the buyer to buy the stakes from Vimal and Ruchi and later from us to gain majority stake holding?" I asked, still reluctant to completely exit from the company that I had built from scratch.

"I doubt. You are, what, around thirty crores today in revenue? A mere twenty five percent holding will not excite a big player. Also, as a friend and well-wisher, let me tell you, if you get a complete exit, you should go ahead and monetize. Or else valuation will only be in paper and in two years, the market may not be so good," Nitish cautioned us.

"I completely agree, Nitish. What do you think could be our valuation?" I asked, curiously

"Depends upon how important your business is for the buyer. How much do you think you would grow in the next two to three years?"

"From thirty odd crores this year to easily the double of what – sixty crores. We can explain the hypothesis if required," Anand said optimistically.

"That sounds really fantabulous, but then there has to be some discounting factors as well. Let me tell you, the valuation could be anywhere around forty crores, roughly 1.3 times of your current revenue," Nitish estimated. "Ah, if we push hard with the realistic projections for the next three years, we could, maybe add another five crores," Nitish shared his opinion.

"I think we should target at least fifty crores considering our growth trajectory. Business is expected to surge as we will be signing three significant contracts with two MNCs and a large Indian IT company shortly," I explained. "If you want us to project our numbers for the next three years, we will do it with the help of a spreadsheet. I am sure we can incorporate acceptable hypothesis and excite the spreadsheet to ejaculate amazing financial numbers. You must have done this for a few of your clients, I bet!"

"Let us work it out like this. We will have forty-five as floor price and push hard for a higher price. Don't worry, guys, I am here to protect your interests and shall get you the best valuation. This requires real hard selling and bargaining, leave it to me," Nitish assured us.

"Bingo! Nitish, have you already identified any prospective buyer? Sorry if I am pushing you too much!" Anand's eagerness was amplified.

"I have one or two on my mind. I shall get back later on this once we agree on our terms and after you give me an exclusive mandate," Nitish meant business.

"What are your terms?" both of us chorused.

"We will keep it at 1.5 percent on the sale value and in case I achieve a valuation of more than fifty crores, an additional 2 percent on the value in excess of fifty crores."

"Is that a fair deal?" I quipped

"I actually charge more, but, for friends like you, I can't do that and you need to trust me."

"Of course we have faith in you. Send us the agreement for the mandate and let's do it," Anand was quick to conclude.

"Nitish, one final question. Do you think we should sell?" I asked him to completely weed out any ambiguity in our minds.

"Yes, the time is ripe to monetize and move on. You guys are young enough to explore other opportunities. When the market knows that you can build and sell companies, you will find investors swarming around you. You may not need me then."

We all laughed aloud and shook hands.

"Nitish, care for a drink this evening?" my offer was spontaneous to celebrate the success of the deal in advance.

"Oh sorry Gautam, I don't drink, but thanks for the invite."

Nitish left our office but Anand and I drove down to a nearby bar to celebrate the deal in advance, as we seldom liked to postpone celebrations.

Avinash Closes the Deal

We updated Vimal and Ruchi about the discussion we had had with Nitish. Both felt that selling the entire company was a better option and that a price upward of even forty crores was good enough. Their confirmation and acceptance was important for us to proceed with the deal in progress. We subtly rejected Vimal's offer to identify a buyer for a professional fee.

Though we were keen to close the deal, a sense of misgiving haunted us each day as the business was growing by leaps and bounds. From where we started, we had since moved to a swanky commercial building and operated a few delivery centres in each of the metros excepting Delhi and Kolkata. We were also getting enquiries from companies outside the country though, in a small way, we were already handling some of the international business of our clients.

Two months after we had the meeting with Nitish, he called us and chose to talk to me.

"Gautam, are you guys in town tomorrow? The good news is that I have identified a buyer for you – a gentleman by name of Deepak Manjrekar, CEO of IndAsia BPO. Avinash from Red Sand India Fund would like to meet you guys as well. Red Sand is a venture capital company," Nitish sounded excited.

"But why a venture capital company? We are not looking for any funds now, we have mandated you to get us a buyer!"

"I know, but this company may fund the buyer further as they already hold some equity in this company. Hence in our own interest, we need to impress Avinash."

"Do you know him? If you know him, we can easily do it I suppose," I said thoughtfully.

"No, I don't know them. For these transactions, it is better to deal with the unknown ones," he explained. "I have already discussed the matter with the CEO of the buyer company and he is quite excited. I just got to know him through a common friend of ours and that's how it works."

"Great, Nitish, looks like we are on the fast track now."

"Yes Gautam, and not to worry, I am here to handle them."

Nitish's assurance gave me a lot of confidence.

The next day Deepak, Avinash and Nitish were at our office. Anand took them through our financials, organization structure, clientele and the details of our leadership team. We also took them to a couple of delivery centres in the city. Deepak was very impressed.

"Your trailblazing growth in such a short span of time is really amazing and it is certainly a story to tell," Deepak showed magnanimity in his compliments.

"Thanks a lot… The irony is that Nitish is trying to sell our company now," I said trying to gauge Avinash's reaction to it.

"Market is good now and selling is all about timing. I strongly feel that your decision is apt. At some point of time, you need to unlock the value and create wealth and there is no better time than now," Avinash's reply was along expected lines.

Deepak narrated the credentials of IndAsia BPO and subtly indicated to us that there were two more companies in the same space as ours that were being considered for acquisition.

"So you need to quickly move in if you are interested, and mind you, this is a 100% cash out deal," the offer from Avinash was exciting as well as added to the pressure. For a few minutes, I was travelling a distance in my dream where I was sitting surrounded by cash of over ten crores, my share of the sale proceeds net of tax. I could retire and do nothing, and even Neha could have the option of quitting her job. Retirement at the age of 35 was a blessing and a heavenly feeling!

"What value are you expecting? If you are uncomfortable to disclose it, leave it to us and we shall revert with our offer," Avinash said, bringing me back to reality.

"We don't have any issues in indicating our expectations, Avinash, either it works or it doesn't. Nitish must have indicated it to you by now. Anywhere in the range of sixty crores would entice us," Anand was greedy by just a few crores, I thought wryly.

"You are at thirty crores and you expect a multiple of over two! That's definitely too much," Avinash clearly agreed with me on that!

"No, look at it. The kind of mandates we have been signing in the recent past clearly will enable us to cross the barrier of fifty crores within the next two years. You may be aware that we are leaders in this space, I mean in the accounting services. With both accounting and pay roll processing services soaring, we are very optimistic. If anything, our expectation is very reasonable," I supported Anand's claim with facts.

"I have clearly explained your strengths and perhaps we would look at something that works for all. At the end of the day, every deal has to be a win-win for both," Nitish said like a true broker.

"We shall come up with our offer though sixty is impossible," Avinash said, giving us the impression that we could easily get fifty plus crores. If we could get anything over fifty-five, it would be a jackpot for us. Considering even Vimal had pegged it only at forty crores plus, this was very promising. The expectation of a passive shareholder would always be lower especially when he had not invested cash or effort, as any realization for such a shareholder was in itself a booty.

"Let's arrive at something that works well for both in the larger interest of the business. Remember, as sellers, FAB can only sell once and hence there should be an exciting offer from your," Nitish concluded on our behalf, looking at Avinash.

"What would be our role post acquisition, unless it is too early to get a commitment from either side?" I asked to be sure that my dream could indeed become a reality.

"I have checked with Deepak. In everybody's interest, you may stay for one year to help in the transition and ensure continuity to your existing clients. Later, they can manage on their own as they have a very capable team," Avinash replied promptly.

"That sounds good. If you want us to continue for even two years, we are prepared. The interest of the company will be of prime importance to us and we don't have any personal ego that would hinder us from turning out to be employees of the company promoted by us. Let's discuss this at an appropriate time," I was emphatic and Anand nodded in agreement.

"So we will proceed with the other formalities including a non-binding term sheet, basic due diligence subject to your acceptance to the valuation to be mentioned in the term sheet," Avinash wanted a reconfirmation

"Please proceed and push the valuation to an acceptable level, after all, we can sell our company only once!" was my final dictum after I borrowed the punch line from Nitish.

Avinash explained the process once again and the timelines for a while and Nitish, on our behalf, committed himself to coordinating the whole deal including the formalities involved in it.

After they left, Anand and I thought that the time was ripe to discuss our post retirement plans. It was a funny and joyful feeling, and at the same time we felt emotional.

ꝺ

FAB for a Fabulous Price

The next three months were hectic. Any new business development was put on hold on account of the new development. While I interacted with Deepak and Nitish regularly, Anand focused on ensuring that the current service levels didn't suffer because of the sale-in-progress.

Deepak was a very aggressive and ambitious entrepreneur. He had the potential to create an empire. He had several great qualities and had absolute clarity in what he wanted. I was also convinced that our excellent team of human resources would progress in their career under his stewardship.

There were exchanges of mails and the terms of the non-binding term sheet were discussed especially on the valuation front. The final value was agreed to a whopping fifty-two crores. Though the final offer didn't match our greed for sixty crores, we yielded to the offer as we were anyways in 'sell mode' and Nitish strongly recommended selling. A board meeting was held to get Vimal and Ruchi's concurrence and pass the resolution for the sale of business at fifty-two crores. We conveyed special thanks officially to Nitish for his exemplary skill and ability to negotiate and get the best deal for us. The board meeting was very cordial as everyone was happy with the obscene amount of money which overshadowed the ugly debates we had had earlier.

"We must congratulate you guys. In just ten years or so, you have created and sold a company for over $9 million USD! For a services company in India, this is an excellent job,"Vimal praised us. His excitement was obvious as his bank balance would swell with the least effort from his end.

"Yea, but given a chance we would have taken the company to one hundred crores and created history," Anand said with immense confidence.

"We know your ability, yet congrats for creating this history," Ruchi patted Anand. Big money filling everyone's pocket seemed to bring back the smiles in the relationships.

"Vimal, let me ask you something openly," I said.

"Oh sure please, shoot!"

"You had indicated a few months ago that valuation of forty crores and more was good enough. Now that we are selling the company for fifty-two crores, would Ruchi and you pay us the excess amount? After all, it was Anand and I who managed to get such a valuation. We feel we deserve to get more and we will also disburse a part of the surplus among our front line managers." I had nothing to lose and then, I was right. Even at forty crores, they would have happily walked away with ten crores for doing nothing or next to nothing and hence I was marginally optimistic that they would be considerate

All fell silent.

"And Vimal, if you see this as ethical and reasonable, we can always rejig our equity structure before the actual transfer of shares happen," I broke the silence with a suggestion on how it could be done in a practical way

"Gautam , don't get me wrong. I think as 25% shareholders, we should get what we are legally entitled to. Let us respect the laws of the land. Moreover, even if he had sold the company for sub forty crores, we wouldn't have claimed anything additional from you just because you sold it for less than the minimum of forty crores I indicated. We would have willingly suffered the notional loss. Also your impatience and inability to stay in business are also the reason for us to exit too soon. If we had opted to build this business for the next two or three years, I am sure we would achieve a valuation of a hundred crores. Your impatience and unprofessionalism is costing me a lot, am losing valuation on this count. Let us be fair, guys."

"But Vimal, Ruchi does business with a few of our clients by providing manpower. Both of you have also invested with a rival company. I think it is really incorrect and unethical. You need to compensate for that, don't you think so?" I still persisted, expecting him to play fair, at least because his conscience pricked.

"Gautam, we have never done anything illegal. Our arrangement never prevented us from exploring new business opportunities even if they seemed to be competing with FAB. Let's talk about what is legal as ethical is too broad a term in business," Vimal the ace businessman said.

"Oh my God, you managed to justify your points of view well. Fine, let us go by legality, no issues. I request again to consider my suggestion as you know very well that this company was built brick by brick by me and Anand."

"Don't forget that we were on the board from the moment you invited us. There is always a huge intrinsic value that should also get rewarded," Vimal countered brilliantly and shamelessly and I must admit that he was too good on that count

"Fine Vimal, I give up," I said, maybe he was not so surprised at that.

"Guys, the success out of this great association calls for a huge celebration. Let's do it tonight," Ruchi, who was on her way to make a cool six crores from FAB, was keen to celebrate. She even opted to host another party in Mumbai where she said we could even invite Deepak, Avinash's boss Jayanth, Avinash, Nitish and a few select clients and other invitees. "Let's do this in Mumbai soon and I shall make the arrangements."

"Sure, we will celebrate soon," I said, wanting to put an end to this celebration.

The entire transaction was finally concluded in the following two months. Deepak had decided to retain most of the old team and such a decision gave us a huge relief as every member of our team had a chance to grow in a larger company. We collectively addressed our team and convinced them that they were now part of a larger group and that it would mean better career opportunities and progression. We also decided that Deepak and I should together meet every important client over a period of two months.

Red Sand funded the buy-out. We transferred the shares in lieu of money and FAB became a subsidiary of IndAsia. Anand and I became quite rich by our own standards. Each of us made a few crores, a sum we wouldn't have imagined we would ever make in our life time. Vimal and Ruchi together made thirteen crores.

Out of the sale proceeds, Anand and I willingly shared a substantial amount with our team members, rewarding those who had been with us for over five years.

The sale of business got reported the very next day in one of the dailies. The brief report was as under:

> *FAB Management Services India P Ltd, a Chennai based Accounting Services company, was acquired by Mumbai based firm IndAsia BPO, a company headed by Deepak Manjrekhar, for an undisclosed amount. When our correspondent spoke to Vimal Chand, who is on the Board of FAB, he mentioned that this was a right move from FAB not only to reward the shareholders but also to leverage the growing opportunities globally through a larger entity like IndAsia. To a question if he would be part of the board of the*

company post acquisition, he mentioned that he could not share such details at this point of time.

Anand threw the paper in disgust. "I am sure Deepak is not such a fool to do what we did," he said.

"Ha ha...forget it man, no pain no gain. It is only thanks to Vimal that we sold our company and made the kind of money we wouldn't have imagined in our life."

"I agree," Anand smiled with some difficulty.

It was agreed that Anand and I would continue with the company for six months, for a salary, of course! Since the migration happened quite smoothly within three months, we suggested that we would move out early and save cost for the company.

At thirty-five years of age, we were without a job but with plenty of money; it was heavenly. In fact, Anand asked me one day "Do we deserve so much money?"

"Can't say, Anand. It is a reward for the risk we took. When the market pays you, there need not be any logic! Learn from Vimal – we are legally entitled to that kind of money." We laughed aloud.

There was happiness on the home front as well. My father told me that he always had the confidence that one day I would make it. I told him to now use the money that he had parked in a fixed deposit for me as reserve money for himself. I also bought a small apartment for my parents in Chennai so that they could move there and live close to me.

Anand's in-laws were very happy and attributed Anand's success to lady luck Divya as she was always considered lucky and her name also included Lakshmi, goddess of wealth. Neha was happy for me but she continued to work as she loved her job.

New Space Leased

After the sale of the company and ourretirement, we enjoyed ourselves for a few days. Anand and I had decided that we would not meet or communicate with each other for three or four weeks. I had opted for a lovely trip to Europe with Neha. And only while holidaying in Europe did we realize that we were becoming parents in a few months.

After coming back from our holiday, I found it very difficult to kill time. After all, Anand and I had spent every day together for the past ten years and that had become very addictive. We spoke to each other and met at Coffee World. We agreed that we had to meet at least once every two days even if there was nothing to do. We hired a small office space for ourselves and it so happened that we started meeting each day religiously as though we had some official work at hand. Yet, it was so relaxing to spend a few hours chatting, talking, browsing and even exploring our next venture with no seriousness attached to it!

Now and then we were busy with a few interviews and bytes for certain financial dailies and magazines. The same media people who never paid any heed to us for any story on FAB when we were building the company were thereafter very keen to tell our tale. Media respected 'selling' more than 'building'. FAB was featured as a cover story in one of the leading business magazines and Anand's picture was on the cover with the story titled "Young Winners, a FABulous story of an enterprise".

Anand told me that Divya had bought one hundred copies of the magazine to be given to their relatives and friends. The cover story carried a detailed interview with Anand. I could not participate in the interview as I was holidaying in Europe. I liked and enjoyed some parts of the interview very much.

Reporter: Did you think when you started that you would be able to build such a company and, more importantly, exit in this fashion?

Anand: Of course, yes. While we were building the company, we had clear vision in creating value for our shareholders. Nobody can visualize the exact exit time and it was the same in our case too. Our exit was made taking into account the interest of our shareholders, our human capital and our clients.

Reporter: Do you think you sold the company a bit too early?

Anand: No way. The timing was perfect. We felt that it was time for us to move on and allow the company to leverage larger opportunities under a bigger and larger brand.

Reporter: You and Gautam were the original promoters. We are sure that other board members Vimal and Ruchi must have played a pivotal role, can you elaborate?

Anand: Enormous. Vimal's strategy and global exposure and Ruchi's astute customer development and retention strategy proved very useful to our company. It was fabulous working with them.

Reporter: Any advice to young budding entrepreneurs?

Anand: Chase your dream with clear plans and sincerity. Don't give up during difficult times. Change is the only constant! Change strategies, plans, processes, technology and people when required. Be good at change management.

Reporter: One big lesson that you learnt.

Anand: Legally being on the right side doesn't mean you are ethically fair and reasonable and vice versa!

"Wow, Anand, what an interview! I loved your reply on 'being legally correct'. That's a super punch!"

"I was fuming when he asked about Vimal and Ruchi but I wanted to be diplomatic," Anand explained.

"That's fine, man. We should thank them throughout our lives, the kind of exit we had is more like a pleasurable pain. Enjoy the pain!"

"Agree totally, yet they are thick-skinned…"

"Forget it, are you now in touch with your friend Ruchi?" I teased Anand.

"Yes, of course," he grinned sheepishly, "but only through Facebook. For your kind information, I have added Avinash as my friend too, so it is clear that I am not tilted towards the fair sex only."

"Ok, I am not passing any judgment, Anand. I know you are pretty good at digital networking."

"Nothing like that, it is just to kill time. For this purpose I have even added a few friends of Ruchi as my friends, real pretty ones. My God, these chicks keep posting their pictures every now and then! Some are damn good, I will show them to you later."

"No thanks, Anand, I am not good at digital dating. Leave me alone!" I pleaded jovially.

"But you must join Facebook, Gautam, it is real fun and at times helpful too. You really connect with many people," Anand recommended seriously.

"I am not cut out for it. I am not keen to make the world know what I am doing. Look at all these posts, they are nauseating; I did this, I went there, I ate this, several pictures with several titles 'with my father', 'with my mother', 'our loving family', 'what a party', 'what are friends for' and several arm chair critics, economists, commentators and people who keep blowing their own trumpets. It is not for me, at least not for the time being."

"Agree buddy, but it will be interesting to find out what others are doing," Anand justified with a joke.

One day, there was a mail from Vimal.

Hi guys,

All well I hope. Life has become too hectic for me. Being a globe trotter is painful at times and adds fatigue. I am now in Boston and am back in India early next month. I am joining the board of a couple of companies based out of Delhi and Mumbai. One is into e commerce and the other is an IT company. This will add further challenges, and I am loving it.

What's up with you guys?You must be getting into your next venture, I bet! It will be my pleasure to help you guys professionally. Let me know if we could have some face time in Mumbai next month. Read the story on FAB in one of the magazines, Anand's interview was top class.

Catch you

Cheers
Vimal

"Shameless creature! Facebook is any day better than these faceless worms," Anand spewed venom.

"Why do you say so? He really believes that he has been useful to us! Why can't you reply, Anand?"

"No way, I have already deleted the mail. I feel sorry for those two companies who are going to induct him into their boards."

"Ha ha...I shall reply to him. There is nothing wrong in replying and staying connected with no strings attached. I hope you don't have any objection to it," I incensed Anand.

"Absolutely no problem, please don't mark a copy to me, that's my only request," he was still unable to forget the bitter past.

I sent a reply to Vimal stating that we hadn't applied our mind to any new venture and that we would definitely consider his offer.

I was learning diplomatic business communication after making some wealth out of business.

Intrigue

"Gautam, where are you? You need to come here now," Anand called me one Saturday morning sounding very agitated.

"Not today," I tried to put him off. "Let's meet on Monday or over a coffee tomorrow," I was not keen to venture out that day.

"Come on, this is urgent! I tried reaching you twice and even sent you a message! I am not a fool to do that unless it is urgent!" Anand said edgily.

"Anything wrong Anand, where are you?"

"I am at the office. Come over as early as possible."

"What's wrong? Tell me now!" I was becoming anxious and annoyed with him.

"Something I found on Facebook," Anand replied and that irritated me even more.

"Bullshit! You and your addiction to Facebook. Bury your face in the recycle bin!"

"Come on, listen! I made a new friend Kavya who is a friend of Ruchi..." he was started to say something when I interrupted.

"I am not interested, Anand. I will be there in an hour's time. I have to complete my chores.

I was annoyed with Anand. I thought he was making a mountain out of a mole hill, and unnaturally obsessed with Ruchi. Why should becoming friends with Kavya cause him so much agony? When I reached office, I found Anand glued to his iPad.

"Sorry Gautam, good that you made it. Look at this, she is Kavya, Ruchi's friend," Anand showed me the girl's Facebook page.

"She is very beautiful and dangerously attractive, but so what?" I exclaimed, unable to take my eyes away from Kavya's picture.

He then clicked the 'photos' in her page and several glamourous pictures opened up one after the other.

Anand clicked one of the thumbnails to reveal a bigger version. It looked like a picture taken at a party. There were three or four sets of photographs posted as Anand was clicking one after the other looking at me. What I immediately noticed was several good looking faces and well-dressed guys and girls.

I could see some familiar faces in the photographs. To our immense surprise, we saw Vimal, Ruchi, Avinash and even Nitish among others in the same picture.

"Look at these cheats, they have always known each other," Anand said accusingly.

"So what, they must have met and partied, and have a right to do so. Don't feel jealous that you were not invited," I tried to soothe him as well as myself. "Anand, stop doubting every move of theirs," I said, wondering if there was something in Anand's suspicion.

"Damn it, all that money has made you soft! Look at the date when the photo was uploaded. This was taken nine months back," Anand pointed out.

I was going through the comments. There were one hundred and forty likes and thirty-five comments.

"Look at the number of 'likes'. Bloody hell, there are hardly five 'likes' for my profile pictures and one of the 'likes' is from Divya's grandmother," he poured out an irrelevant lament on the side.

The comments below the photographs were mysterious.

"Great party....great pair"

"hot pair"

"what a party, thanks to Avi and Ruchi, you guys rock"

We went through the entire album and came across one picture where Avinash was kissing Ruchi on her cheeks and there were many 'likes' and comments. Anand would have been the only person who disliked the picture, given an option.

One of the comments gave us enough material.

"five years of romance, now getting engaged, happy for you Avi and Ruchi"

Nitish was seen in a picture with his arms around the shoulders of Avinash and Ruchi.

"So this is the reason for your anger and anguish, I can understand."

"We have been taken for a ride, Gautam. All these guys are part of the team; they are a shoal of fish from the same pond and the pond stinks," Anand's anger was raising the mercury level in the room.

"Very clear that they didn't want to reveal these facts earlier to us," I said.

"But then, why? Can you guess?" Anand queried, wanting to know what I thought.

I took fifteen minutes to connect all the dots.

"Look, it could be like this. All of them had planned to get something out of our company and they must have designed the plan a few months back. Firstly, all of them have definitely been friends for a while now and that includes your senior CA friend Nitish. Ruchi and Avinash have been dating each other for years and they were planning to marry sometime soon. After the relationship between us and them became strained a few months back, they must have resolved to use their network not only to safeguard their interests but also gain substantially through various means," I narrated with conviction.

"What do you mean by safeguarding their interests? In any case they are shareholders who would gain naturally…" Anand was mystified.

"Totally, yet, they must have feared that we would have slowed down the process of selling or messed up the opportunities that would have come our way," I was explaining their motive as if I was also a party to the entire plot.

"How could they benefit, I don't understand," Anand was confused.

"Simple Anand, it is just that they saw an opportunity and they grabbed it. They may not have planned this from day one, but when certain things came together, they would have strategized to make use of it for their collective benefit."

"Go on," Anand asked curious.

"Avinash must have identified IndAsia. He would have heard about us through Vimal. Nitish being your friend gave them a leverage to negotiate their terms. Vimal must have asked him to interact with us independently."

"Wow, and benefit from the deal!" Anand jumped in.

"Child's play, Anand. Nitish made eighty lakhs from us and may have earned something from IndAsia through Avinash. Though a broker doesn't get rewarded by both the parties, these guys could have built it into the deal without either Deepak or us suspecting it." I continued thoughtfully, "For Avinash, this is a big deal and he would have cemented his position apart from any monetary incentive he would have earned."

"Carry on," Anand listened in rapt attention.

"Look at the huge short term gain. Whatever Ruchi got from us, and we know it is over five hundred lacs, will shortly become their family money. How many can dream to have such financial liquidity when you are just married?"

"Bingo! Your detections are outstanding. Carry on," Anand said sounding more excited than angry.

"Vimal has easily pocketed close to eight hundred lakhs for doing literally nothing. Nitish also must have given Avinash if not to all these guys a cut from whatever he earned. Am I right?" I concluded with a great sigh.

"Oh fuck! We have been robbed and fooled. I feel ashamed as these guys have taken us for a royal ride! But they could have told us they knew each other. We would have just grinned and nodded,"

Anand strongly felt that they could have revealed the facts as we were going ahead with the sale plan no matter what. Anand was visibly upset at our naivety.

"Come on buddy, they know us too well. We wouldn't have budged had we known these facts. We would have smelt a rat and would have hindered the progress and messed up the whole thing," I believed in our astuteness.

"Buddy, I think we should let them know that we know everything. Let them feel bad and regret," Anand said in a childlike stubbornness.

"You think they will feel bad and regret? Only now you are talking like a fool Anand. They will just laugh and celebrate our discovery and they will party harder."

Anand mulled over it silently and said slowly, "I think you are right."

"I am not saying don't write," I said, now that I knew he had given up that idea, "but just that you will achieve nothing! They resorted to making money in a quick and smart way. They don't operate the way you and I do. They are not emotional fools like us. They are right in their own way," I tried convincing Anand, convincing myself in the process.

"Let's confess that they are street smart, they knew to play their cards very well and close to their chest. We must still whole heartedly thank them as we also made more money than we expected. They bargained for a great price for their profit, but helped us in the process," I tried to find the silver lining.

"Look, we are good at building a company and running it successfully with the right people, process, resources and methods. Vimal is good in identifying the opportunities in these companies and through some perceived contribution, encashes something to his advantage and his agenda may also bring rewards to the other stakeholders. Ruchi is an extension of Vimal. Avinash is a greedy guy and like any self-centered corporate manager, plays his role and the industry he is associated with also suits his outlook as he is able to exploit it. Nitish is a broker; all he does is connect with people for his own gains. He manages the egos of the people on both sides as the middleman. He is not bothered about how the relationship on the brokered deal progresses once his coffers are filled," I elaborated.

"Who is the loser then?"

"No one, in this case, at this moment. Five years from now, we will know if someone loses. That also depends on how IndAsia manages and grows the business and the market condition at that point of time. Now if you ask me, each of us has benefitted and all are winners."

"But this is not the way one wins!" Anand needed some more convincing.

"It's like this... In a cricket match, a team is at times declared winner based on the Duckworth Lewis method. It may look weird but a winner is a winner on record."

"All fine, yet the feeling of feeling fooled is terrible," admitted Anand.

"Never feel like that. Tell the world that you were a huge success... that's the world view and you need to live with it. Remember, no one wants to hear about your failure. Success has many ears," I said sagely.

'And lastly Anand, your romance with Facebook did help us unearth some mystery but let us not dig the mud beyond this. Life has much more to offer, so cheer up man."

Both of us were relieved, distressed and extremely pleased with ourselves.

ᔕ

Three Months Later

We had exited from FAB completely and the company had merged with IndAsia BPO. We had nothing to do except explore various investment opportunities with the money we had made.

Anand had already become a proud father of a daughter and he was getting wishes including some consoling ones from some of his relatives assuring him that his next child would be a baby boy! Anand's joy seemed to be sorrow for a few others in the family. So he itched to create something again.

Neha and I were expecting our first child in the coming two months. We were still debating whether she should continue working or quit. I offered to take care of the child so she could continue to work as she loved it so much.

One evening Anand and I met at the Bikes and Barrels bar at Residency Towers. We were on the pretext of discussing our next venture over a drink.

"So what's next?" I asked Anand just to make conversation.

"You tell me, chief. Left to me, I don't want to do anything very serious," replied Anand as he went through the wine card.

"Come on, we haven't done anything serious. It is just that what we did turned out to be serious business," I jested.

We laughed and ordered some whiskey.

'Anand, there are two options. One, we just get into some business or venture and carry on with it just to keep ourselves occupied. No room for budgets, forecasts, endless and meaningless presentations and, more importantly, no third party stepping in. The new venture exists with us and dies when we he hit the grave. The second one is to leverage our credentials now. We know how the market behaves, how investors look at business and how the business world will look at us. We can play the game of business again and create something out of nothing. What do you say?" I thought this proposition would interest Anand.

Just then we saw Nitish walking in with a few people into the bar. He was genuinely excited to see us. He introduced us to his companions.

"We have heard about you from Nitish. Nitish has told stories about you and you were lucky to get a consultant like him. Now we are banking on his advice, which he is kind enough to offer," one of them said.

Anand suppressed his laughter and coughed instead. He was perhaps thinking, "We have a story to tell too."

They went to their table but Nitish stayed back to chat with us.

"Nitish, you don't drink, so what brings you here?" I asked purposely.

"Occupational hazards, what to do! I have to give these guys some advice on a business deal. I am helping them set up a power plant in Tamil Nadu," he was full of pride.

"Wow, I didn't know you were knowledgeable about the power sector!" Anand pretended to be awed.

"As consultants, we need to learn about every industry," Nitish replied coolly.

"Have a drink, man! When you are in a bar, you cannot down fresh lime and soda while others sip liquor… unless that's the right way of handling your business," Anand commented and laughed.

"What next, guys? Let me know if I can help you in any way…" Nitish offered his services again.

I winked at Anand subtly and replied, "Nitish, we are now looking at agro business. That's the business of the future."

"Wow, can you explain briefly?" Nitish was all ears.

"In simple terms, we are looking at deployment of cutting edge neo technology, infrastructure and process where perhaps the end price of potatoes, for instance, to the end consumer could go down from the current Rs 30 to somewhere around Rs 10 or so," I blabbered weaving all the buzzwords together.

"Great, man! We will meet soon on this. Now you have to excuse me," Nitish left with a bounce in his step and joined his guests.

"Look at this joker! Tonight he will be all over Google to know all about potatoes and the technologies deployed across the world. He will very soon start yapping about it to many," I couldn't control my laughter.

"Will he?" Anand was laughing

"Yes, professional hazards," I said and we laughed some more.

We laughed aloud and hit a high five (again 'five')

"Come on Gautam, tell me seriously, what next?" Anand asked with more interest.

"One double large for each of us," I said.

Again there was spirited laughter. Though somewhere a new business was brewing.